THE RAG TRADE

A Star Original

'A thousand pounds is a small investment to see my firm become an international gown manufacturer.'

'It may seem small to you,' said Mr Thickitt reasonably. 'But then we don't owe you £45,000 do we? . . . 't your mother-in-law help?'

Fenner shuddered and looked roun hiding in a filing cabinet or something. Th king her for money induced him to n the decanter on the bank man ar-dried throat and croak

'Many people have ked the bank manager.

Fenner though ager taking it on the chin, but

'I don't think it hel Mr Thickitt sympathetically.

Peter Buchanan

Ronald Wolfe's and Ronald Chesney's

THE RAG TRADE

Based on the successful
London Weekend Television series

A STAR BOOK
published by
The Paperback Division of
W. H. ALLEN & Co. Ltd

A Star Book
Published in 1977
by the Paperback Division of
W. H. Allen & Co. Ltd
A Howard and Wyndham Company
44 Hill Street, London W1X 8LB

Printed in Great Britain by
Cox & Wyman Ltd., London, Reading and Fakenham

ISBN 0 352 30110 4

CHAPTER ONE

Fenner gripped the handle of the axe tighter, making his knuckles turn white, as stealthily he crept up behind his wife; he was about to strike a blow for freedom, his freedom. All the nagging would be shut off instantly, like an un-plugged television. Slowly he raised the axe, his wife still unaware, a snarling sneer began to invade his face as his whole body tensed for the mortal blow.

'Did you hear what I said?' asked his wife. 'You sit there half in a dream, you never hear what I say.' Her words rushed Fenner back to reality as he shuffled in his chair, to give the impression that he *was* paying attention to her. He was startled to find her standing in front of him, instead of lying on the floor in a pool of blood with a huge axe embedded in her skull. Self-consciously he fidgeted with his hands as though hurriedly hiding his unused and imaginary axe. 'Yes dear,' he murmured, showing he was awake, even over breakfast.

Fenner, a youngish looking man in his fifties, was a peaceful man inside; his only problem was the outside world. He owned Fenner Fashions, a small gown-making factory in the East End which, again inside, he enjoyed very much, but outside he had two immediate problems – a £45,000 bank overdraft and a mother-in-law who had put up the money for Fenner Fashions. His dream had been realized some years ago when after a lifetime in the rag trade, he met and married a beautiful young model with money – well, her mother's money really. But he persevered and his happy marriage eventually prised the backing money for Fenner Fashions from his mother-in-law, she having lent him the money to cement the marriage. Unfortunately, the problems began when the cement dried and became a huge immovable block around his marital neck. Naturally, any man with such worries usually finds his own sanctuary by immersing himself totally in his work, in his case at the factory, but even in that quiet lair lay a tiger in the shadows; her name was Paddy, the shop steward for Fenner Fashions. She, a girl in her thirties, had missed her vocation according to Fenner. She should never just be a humble shop steward in a small factory, he thought. Her real destiny should be the guiding hand behind the industrial problems of ICI or China. How he prayed she would one day follow her destiny.

'If you were a more aware person,' his wife continued, 'you would be a more successful man. When I was a full-time practising model, I took no notice of anyone. Oh, they all tried to tell me what to do, but I refused to listen, I just turned a deaf ear, to them all, and blazed a trail of success to the top.'

Fenner's hands reached for his imaginary axe, but then thought of the mess on his new carpet which hadn't been paid for yet and relaxed his grip. 'You don't have the worry of all the girls at the factory – every day they demand something,' he said in defence.

'Then you should stand up to these women, fight back,' his wife said, doing exactly what she was advising him not to do. '*I've* been in the trade, and I know what they get up to, and now they're a damn sight better off than I am.'

The 'German fighter bomber' droned on as Fenner listened to his ranting wife. 'They get far too much money,' she continued, 'and all because you're weak. You take too many orders from them – get me the toast,' she interrupted herself. 'It's about time you took a tougher line with those women, refused a bit more often – go and call mother,' she ordered.

As Fenner's mother-in-law entered the breakfast room, he quickly buried himself in the financial pages of his newspaper. He read the opposite page. *Woman Boiled Alive in Chocolate* said the headline. 'I wonder how many bars it would take to fill our bath,' he thought and then added another thought, nodding good morning to his mother-in-law. 'Twice.'

'Get mother her hot chocolate,' his wife demanded. He dropped the paper in terror.

'It was only a thought,' he said in astonishment. 'Oh, yes, of course,' he corrected himself, after the shock of feeling these women could read his thoughts.

'Thank you, dear,' said his mother-in-law as he placed the cup and saucer of hot chocolate before her, trying hard not to think at all in case he was discovered.

'Well, I must get off to the factory,' he said, hoping to avoid further confrontation with his mentors. ' 'Bye, dear,' he said, as he moved to kiss his wife on the head. He looked first in case there was any blood, then from the corner of his eye he saw his mother-in-law reach for the financial section of the newspaper. 'I'd better hurry,' he said, edging towards the door. His mother-in-law unfolded the newspaper; Fenner opened the door; his mother-in-law began to read; he was almost out of the door when he heard it. 'Harold!' His mother-in-law's voice froze him in a posture of escape. 'Have you seen this bit in the paper about bank interest rates?'

Trying to kill the conversation he said, 'Oh yes, I've read it all.'

'Well,' said his wife. 'Doesn't it have an effect on our small bank loan?'

'No,' replied Fenner shakily. 'Our small loan will hardly be affected.'

'I don't know,' said the first inquisitor. 'I shouldn't have thought £8,000 was exactly small.' 'Well,' said Fenner, still at the door. 'It is in the big world of business, but not at our level.'

'Rock bottom,' commented his wife sourly.

'Because,' his mother-in-law contributed, 'they are going to charge more for long standing loans . . . how long has our loan been standing?'

Fenner cringed at her reference, making it all sound like a cold cup of tea. 'Now, now,' he said confidently. 'Everything's in hand . . . and I must really get off to the factory . . . er . . . I'm expecting a very important export order and I want to be on hand to attend to it.'

'And make sure you attend to those demanding women as well,' added his wife. 'Oh, and by the way, on your way home tonight, call in at my hairdresser's and ask if my new wig is ready, and if so, bring it home.'

'Very well dear, 'bye now,' said Fenner, thinking 'I'll make sure the wig is axe-proof as well.'

'Oh,' said his mother-in-law, just as he reached the front door. 'Bring me a *Financial Times*, will you Harold?'

As Fenner drove to the factory, he could feel his anger rising within. 'Damn cheek,' he said aloud. 'Interfering women. Why can't they let me get on with it in my own way?' He thought no man should have a wife and mother-in-law and a woman shop steward all in one lifetime. Why couldn't they be spread out like other taxes? A middle-aged woman with a pram swore at him as he drove past; he hadn't noticed her pushing her pram between two parked vehicles until the last minute, then just swerving he missed her pram and drove on. 'Silly cow,' he mouthed at her through the window. 'What sort of a highway code does she have? For women with prams – first push the pram on to the road – if it's smashed out of your hands by a passing container lorry, then it's not safe to cross.' He drove on, more alert now. 'I'll show 'em,' he said aloud. 'I'll show all these women – I'll show the world – yes, me – Harold J. Fenner Esquire, Rag Trade Empire Builder, if only they'd let me have all the money—' He slammed his brakes on hard as a pretty young miss stepped off the kerb in front of him. 'My fault entirely,' he smiled, allowing her to cross the road in front of him. He watched her wiggly bottom as it passed and was only disturbed by a rude hoot from the lorry behind. It broke his concentration and he attended to driving his car again. His gloom reasserted itself as he drove on, thinking about his own aggravating women relations. 'It's a conspiracy, women and money,' he said aloud. 'They use it like sex – let you have it with clauses – it's a wonder they don't add VAT.'

He drove through the busy traffic which made it difficult to concentrate on his thoughts; his mind raced along for he knew that with his particular financial situation, something must soon be done, but what? The bank overdraft was £45,000 but he had told his mother-in-law it was only £8,000. Also, he knew she would soon want to know how the affairs of the company in which she had invested were prospering. How could he increase business to put the firm back on a more sound financial footing? If his wife or mother-in-law discovered his difficulty they would want blood – his blood. They'd kill him – definitely kill him. He shuddered at the thought. There would be no question of merely leaving a loaded revolver in his room for him to do the honourable thing – more likely they would nag him into madness for eternity, or even further. He reconsidered the revolver; it was easier – that would really thwart their evil plans. He thought again. No, not the gun. The way his luck was running, he would put it to his head, pull the trigger and miss. He doodled on in his mind. 'How about if I shot all my problems and then myself? No – when my turn came I'd have probably run out of bullets!' Fenner was getting cold with the fear of discovery, his spine felt like an ice lolly – it got worse as he drove along. Every car that followed him might contain either his wife or mother-in-law or both. He glanced in his rear mirror at the car behind. Was that sailor with a beard really his mother-in-law? Same eyes, beady. Same nose, muzzeltof. Studying the sailor nearly caused him to ram the back of the car in front. His mouth was getting dry. Everybody seemed to be staring at him and they all bore a resemblance to his wife or mother-in-law. The lollipop man smiled at him. If he'd been wearing ear-rings Fenner would have sworn that it was his mother-in-law. 'No, it couldn't be – she doesn't have a white coat.' He finally arrived at the car park behind the factory, crouching so low in his seat that it looked as though only his head was driving the car. The car door opened and he slithered snake-like through the back door of the factory; closing it behind him, he stood in the shadows listening for his pursuers as one cold bead of sweat formed on his brow – that was all he could afford, he thought.

'There you are,' said a voice in the dark.

Fenner almost screamed 'Sanctuary.'

'No, Tony,' came the reply. 'Oh,' said a trembling Fenner, 'Tony ... er ... I thought you were a woman ... er ... I mean a sailor ... oh,' ended Fenner, regaining his cool in front of Tony, his workroom cutter. He was the boss now, and had to act accordingly in front of his employees. 'I've had one of those mornings – the driving in the traffic gets me agitated.' They walked together to Fenner's office, where he sat behind the desk in his moderately furnished office and Tony stood before him. Tony was quite a good-looking young man in his late twenties with modern hair-style and clothes under a workroom apron. He had been with Fenner Fashions some time and was a good cutter in the trade, but in addition to being a cutter he was something of a confidante of Fenner, almost an acting foreman, unpaid of course. Like the young man he was, Tony spoke with reality in his dealings with Fenner, whilst Fenner talked back in what seemed a strange way, because Fenner always had the boss's view of things and didn't always tell Tony of the schemes in his older mind.

'We've had a bit of trouble here this morning with one of the girls and Paddy wants to see you,' said Tony, outright.

Nervously, Fenner reached for his Alka-Seltzer, which seemed to fizz much louder this morning. 'What's wrong now?' he asked, sipping the fizzing Seltzer.

'Olive's belt's broken,' said Tony.

'Well can't she use braces?' retorted Fenner with a Seltzer-fizzed nose.

'No, Mr Fenner,' corrected Tony. 'The belt on Olive's machine is broken.'

'Didn't you fix it then?' said Fenner, replacing the glass on his desk.

'Yes, of course,' Tony said tiresomely.

'Then where's the trouble?' burped Fenner.

'It's Paddy. She wants to talk to you about your old and out-of-date sewing machines,' returned Tony, awaiting a reply that might be rude.

'Out-of-date my foot – I've had them for years – they're never out-of-date when there's a good bonus or piece-work job attached to them – then they run hot.'

'Anyway, Paddy wants to see you – so I've given you the message.'

'OK,' said Fenner, rising from his chair. 'I'll be out in a minute.'

'They've all stopped work,' added Tony. 'All right, I'll come out now,' said Fenner annoyed. 'Women, I've got 'em from both sides,' he said as he made his way out of his office to the sewing room, followed by Tony. The sewing room was a good-sized, long room, but with all the equipment that had been squeezed into it, it was obviously not big enough.

Down the centre of the room stood a wide sturdy bench which held two lines of heavy industrial sewing machines with a fluorescent light over each – the girls sat facing each other behind their individual machines, and filling the room around and behind them stood metal-railed racks holding dresses, gowns, skirts, and so on, in various stages of completion. At one end of the room a dirty window allowed a little light to fight its way in and helped keep out some of the traffic noise from the busy street below. A doorway on one side led to a small stockroom, lit only by a single light bulb, operated with a pull string. Fenner strode into the workroom, his steps padded by the multitude of cottons and rag-trade dross tossed from the work bench on to the floor. He offered a sneering smile of 'Good morning, girls, as he stood before them.

A few mumbled, 'Good morning Mr Fenner,' which was

pierced by a firm, 'Ah Mr Fenner,' from Paddy the shop steward.

Fenner's axe hand tightened. He forced a castor-oil smile at Paddy and asked, 'Now Paddy, what seems to be the trouble?'

Paddy turned a stern face towards Fenner, whose words sounded like those of the family doctor to his first morning surgery patient. 'I've ordered a work stoppage,' said Paddy, enjoying it.

'Yes,' said Fenner, his smile draining from his face. 'So I see.'

'I wish to make this stoppage represent a formal complaint about these ancient machines we are forced to use, and as shop steward of Fenner Fashions . . .' she thought what next to say in her official tone, but could not think of anything so merely snarled, 'So what are you going to do about them?'

Fenner splayed his hands, cracked open his face with a smile and said, 'Well – ladies – these are stringent times; the government has had to take stringent measures, and so have I.'

Paddy, disappointed with Fenner's standby excuse, struck her adamant pose. 'Very well, Mr Fenner, this now becomes a stringent strike,' and with that she blew her official strike whistle. The piercing scream of the whistle curdled Fenner's Alka-Seltzer, its sound he well knew to be one of defiance and determination and he cursed the very pea in the whistle. He searched his brain quickly for a suitable lie, then said confidently, 'Girls, as you may know, I was a little late this morning, and there is a very good reason.'

'Not the alarm clock again?' piped Kathy.

'No,' said Fenner, as though a party youngster had misguessed his wrapped birthday gift. 'I have, this very morning, been with the very representative who supplies sewing machines, and we've had a long talk.'

'Really,' said Paddy, waiting.

'I had a long talk with my boyfriend last night,' giggled Kathy, 'but I didn't buy an oil rig.'

Fenner fought to hold his smile as all the girls tittered. Then he looked at Kathy, a girl in her late twenties given, thought Fenner, to outbursts of inane chatter and remarks of the typical dumb-blonde pattern and blessed with only one or two things in her favour – Big Boobs, the reason, thought Fenner, for attracting her rich oil-rig worker boyfriend. 'Quite,' continued

Fenner, glaring at Kathy with a look that would have normally stunned a charging buffalo.

Paddy interrupted his next breath and said bluntly, 'Are we to get new machines or not?'

'The man is coming to see me next week,' Fenner said impatiently – this time without a smile.

'Very well,' said Paddy to Fenner. She turned to the girls and added, 'You have heard a categorical statement from Mr Fenner's own lips that new machines are under negotiation now.'

Fenner opened his mouth to speak, but Paddy's piercing whistle for the resumption of work stopped the breath which Fenner needed. As the machines whirred to a start, Fenner's open mouth remained static as he turned away and left the workroom with the giggling and chattering of the victorious girls drumming on his departing ears.

The resumption of work by the factory girls brought on the usual intermittent whirr of the machines, punctuated by their chatty conversation to a background of *Music While You Work*. Generally, the girls worked quite happily in this busy atmosphere which helped to dilute their very repetitious trade. The garment pieces having been cut into their respective shapes and sizes by Tony, were now strewn on the work bench, but chosen with expertise by the girls to be sewn together, piece by piece, often at different machines by different girls. To the layman this mode of working seemed chaotic, but the completed garments hanging on rails gave proof of the girls conjoined ability and speed.

'Coo, remember that tune,' said Olive, a not too bright girl in her late thirties, to Paddy next to her, as the radio played an 'Oldy'.

'I'm trying to forget it,' said Paddy. 'It reminds me of my age.'

'Oh, I do,' said Olive dreamily. 'They were playing it the night my husband proposed.'

Lynn, a good-looking young girl of nineteen, paused from her work and dreamed also. 'Oh, how romantic. You have your very own song to remember *that* night,' she said to Olive.

'She'd have probably remembered it anyway,' said Paddy with a wink to Mabel, the eldest 'girl' at fifty-five and a staid spinster.

'How do you mean?' said Mabel.

'Well, you don't know what Olive's husband proposed, do you?' replied Lynn with a voice of innocence.

'It must have been good,' added Kathy with a giggle. 'She's still got the smile on her face.'

'Well a little of what you fancy does you good,' chipped in Jo-Jo opposite Olive, as she stuffed a cream bun into her mouth.

'What you fancy's not doing you good,' said Paddy, looking at the bun disappear. 'You're putting on weight again.'

'Oh, that doesn't matter – it gives my husband more to cuddle.' Jo-Jo licked the last creamy black finger.

'But costs him more to feed,' said Mabel a little sourly.

'Well, they can live on love,' chirped Kathy.

'Yes,' said Paddy with a smile. 'All that living – and no washing up.'

Fenner moved away from the window, thinking that one storey wasn't high enough to fling himself out of; he'd probably only break a leg or something, fall on a passing pram and be sued for aerial assault by the doting parents of a flat infant. There was something about prams he thought. Women often pushed them like a rod of office. Perhaps that's what his wife needed, he thought, a good . . .

'Mail,' said Tony as he entered and left the office in a circular walk, dropping the letters on Fenner's desk in passing.

Fenner followed Tony's walk in silence, he was never sure about that boy – whether he would just work quietly for Fenner, or even more quietly take over Fenner Fashions. He strode to his desk in defiance and sat down, reaching for the mail. 'No one was taking over Fenner Fashions,' he thought, and then thought, 'No one would with such an overdraft.'

It is funny how gloom can deepen on a man's face in stages, as one opens bill after bill, like being joltingly lowered into a dark pit. The large envelope carried a patriotically coloured 'Buy British' insignia blazed along the top of the envelope, overpowering Harold J. Fenner, Esq., Director, Fenner Fashions. He studied it for a while, thinking how nice it would be if it had screamed 'Buy Fenner'. Opening the letter he extracted a large type-written letter with elaborate headings at the top. *Bootles of Southampton* it announced proudly. *The*

South's Departmental Store. Fenner remembered the name. He supplied them with clothes. Eagerly he read on, at the same time fearing his contract with them had expired. As he read, his face reacted – he was being raised from a dark pit. *We have arranged a Buy British exhibition for three days in the Civic Hall, Southampton. As you may know, many foreign visitors from Norway, France, Holland, Germany, Belgium, etc., take day trips to Southampton by sea ferries on shopping sprees. Also, being near to a major trans-Atlantic ocean terminal, customers from all over the world shop in Southampton. It is our intention to increase our overseas sales through these customers; hence our exhibition, and we cordially invite Fenner Fashions to supply and man a stand in the exhibition hall, where direct sales to customers would make fine publicity for our wares. If you are interested, please contact us immediately and we can make final arrangements.*

Fenner reached for the phone; he'd read *Yours* . . . at the bottom of the letter, but didn't care if it had been sincerely, faithfully or truly – he read it as *Yours in your great hour of need.* 'Fenner Fashions International – Retail', the doodle on Fenner's telephone pad almost shouted the words with a vocal and trumpet chorus of heavenly music. In a few short minutes his whole body had been transformed from a round-shouldered gown manufacturer, to an upright Zeus, who could hurl thunderbolts of gown creations around the entire world. His dreams were without limit. 'I shall bring Fenner Fashions to the masses of the far world,' he said aloud. 'And you Jose, though you are in Peru riding your humble donkey, you will be resplendent in your Fenner Fashions Poncho.' Collecting the details of the forthcoming exhibition from his telephone pad, he made his way to the workroom to announce, the whole safeguarded future of Fenner Fashions to his very own workers, upon whose shoulders lay the great faith in Fenner to keep them and their families and their pets in full employment.

'We're not going,' said Paddy, almost before the pea in her whistle had stilled after the 'stop work' blast had been blown. Fenner's initial jubilance at announcing the firm-saving exhibition to his workers fell to his socks. Wall Street had crashed in his very own workroom. World War III had been lost at the sound of those three short humble words.

'What do you mean?' he said tearfully to Paddy, 'we're not going?'

'Just that,' said Paddy, accepting nods of accord from the other girls gathered around the workroom table. Fenner steadied himself against a gown rack and then quickly felt the fight returning to his body. He'd fought before for Fenner Fashions, he'd even married for Fenner Fashions, and he reasoned he wasn't going through all that marital purgatory just to cast it aside casually when he stood on the brink of success. He pulled himself up to his full height and gave the girls a lengthy discourse on the whole state of affairs of Fenner Fashions. Desperation drove him to eloquence, he outlined that greater outlets for his merchandise meant more wages – better quality work, a trade name to be proud of, Fenner Fashions International. They would be the first to offer to customers alterations on the spot, a mile-stone in the rag trade. Their creations would be worn throughout Europe, taken there by the foreign visitors that would pack the exhibition and buy Fenner Fashions. This would be their finest hour.

'How much are you paying for this finest hour?' interrupted Paddy.

Fenner, who had been lost in a genuine plea for survival, immediately sensed a crack in the defiant, 'We're not going.' 'Well of course this will be open to negotiation.'

'All right,' said Paddy. 'Let's negotiate.'

'What now?' said Fenner. 'Yes,' answered Paddy equally short. 'Right now.'

'Then you agree to go?' said Fenner placing the thin edge of the bargaining in place.

'Well, it is for Britain,' said Jo-Jo, 'and I'm all for supporting our Empire.'

Fenner wondered if Africa was part of 'our Empire', but was glad of Jo-Jo's support and kindled her interest with a peck on her beaming black face.

'Kisses won't pay the rent,' said Paddy sternly.

'Oh I don't know,' said Kathy. 'That girl in the flat above does all right.'

When the laughter had abated, Paddy outlined the deal. 'We want all expenses paid, including food, fares and hotels.'

'Of course,' agreed Fenner, already working out how he could save money on their expenses.

'And we want an alterations bonus as well,' urged Paddy.

'Here,' said Fenner naturally. 'You won't all be doing alterations.'

'Then we'll take it in turns,' said Paddy, countering Fenner's thrust with her well thought out parry.

'All right,' relented Fenner finally.

'Will we be making dresses for a lot of foreigners?' asked Jo-Jo, proud of her British connections.

'Why yes, of course,' answered Fenner, hoping they would bite further on the benefits of the trip.

'A very good point Jo-Jo,' said Paddy.

Fenner shot her a glance, wondering what his antagonist would find in such an innocent statement.

'Because,' continued Paddy, 'we shall want to know all the exchange rates of their money to work out ours.'

'I don't know what all these exchange rates are,' pleaded Fenner.

'Then you'll have to find out, so we can work out our rates for the different jobs,' said Paddy defiantly.

'Look,' assured Fenner. 'You'll all be paid in English money, so you'll know exactly what you've got.'

'Ah!' said Kathy, 'but our pound is at a low level.' Everyone looked at Kathy, amazed by her profundity. 'Well isn't it?' she asked doubtfully.

'We shall want the *Financial Times* every day,' suggested Mabel.

'Yes,' agreed Paddy, 'so we can keep a daily check on the gold market.'

'Now why don't you stop worrying all of you?' interrupted Fenner. 'It'll be a lovely trip, a few days by the seaside, what better?'

'I thought Southampton was a dock-side' said Lynn innocently.

'Well it's water isn't it?' said Fenner angrily.

'I'm not going paddling in any docks,' said Olive after thinking about it. 'You never know what you might catch.'

'You might catch a sailor,' said Kathy with a saucy grin.

'My old man would be pleased,' thought Olive aloud.

'Why, does he like sailors?' said Lynn.

'Ladies, please,' battled Fenner. 'Everything will be fine for you all.'

'It might be fine for us but I don't know what their husbands might say,' said Paddy nodding to Jo-Jo and Olive.

'What would your old man do, Olive?' said Jo-Jo.

Olive looked up. 'He'd probably pay my fare.'

The girls laughed, but Fenner came in quickly and seriously, 'Would he?'

The negotiations dragged on, and to Fenner it was like having teeth out minus an anaesthetic, because he had to give quite a lot away which pained him. However, he got them all to agree to go: the girls, Tony and himself being the total party. Fenner agreed that he would pay all their expenses and make all the arrangements himself, and in that way none of his money would be paid to the 'Southampton Hilton' as the girls would have it, were there such a hotel to be had.

Over the next few days, the girls worked reasonably happily now they had the prospect of a 'few days by the sea', though Paddy had reservations as always – how she and the girls would fare under the terms that Fenner would 'make all the arrangements'. However, the girls had completed theirs and this became the uppermost talking point above the busy din of the workroom.

'My mum and dad said I must stay with you all the time, Olive,' said Lynn. 'They said because you are married and sensible.'

The girls laughed, and more so when Paddy added, 'Well she's married anyway.'

'What d'you mean?' asked Olive, not catching on.

'She means if you had any sense you wouldn't have got married,' laughed Kathy, helping out.

'Yes that's right,' said Olive, innocently.

'Does your young man mind you going, Kathy?' said Mabel as she finished a long run on her machine.

'He hasn't got much option,' answered Kathy. 'He's stuck out on an oil rig in the North Sea.'

'Well you can send him a love letter from the South Sea,' said Paddy with a grin as she completed her part of a garment.

'Can't you put it in a bottle?' said Olive seriously.

'What he wants won't go in a bottle,' Kathy said as she rolled her eyes.

'I still think we all ought to stick together,' said Lynn, 'in case we get attacked.'

'Speak for yourself,' said Paddy. 'I don't want you lot around if I get attacked.'

'I said she was selfish,' said Kathy. 'She won't share anything.'

Thc happy banter of the girls in the workroom did not reach the ears of Fenner, who was sitting, looking very dejected, in his bank manager's office.

'You see Fenner,' said Mr Thickitt the bank manager, 'you don't seem to realize you are already very much overdrawn and a further loan is quite impossible.'

Fenner looked up forlornly. 'Huh,' he thought. 'This jumped-up youngster is only trying to impress his head office.' He went on, 'They come here, and because they've got a wife and two kids, one of each of course, and a cocker spaniel, they think that everything in their garden's rosy. Just wait till his head office finds out that Fenner has become a multi-millionaire and has transferred his account. The cocker spaniel will get a kick up the rear for a start.' Finally Fenner spoke. 'A thousand pounds is a small investment to see my firm become an international gown manufacturer.'

'It may seem small to you,' said Mr Thickitt reasonably. 'But then we don't owe you £45,000 do we?'

Fenner took a more intense dislike to the cocker spaniel.

'Can't your mother-in-law help?'

Fenner shuddered and looked round in case she was hiding in a filing cabinet or something. The very thought of asking her for more money induced him to take a drink of water from the decanter on the bank manager's desk. He quenched his fear-dried throat and croaked, 'No.'

'Many people have to take it on the chin Fenner,' joked the bank manager.

Fenner thought of the prospect of the bank manager taking it on the chin, but tried another ruse deep from his skulduggerous mind.

'I don't think it helps to cry,' responded Mr Thickitt sympathetically.

Fenner took it that he was very unimpressed by the ploy and couched himself back to reality.

'Have you nothing else as collateral?' chanced Mr Thickitt.

'I could sell the vital organs of my body,' ventured Fenner. 'They do it in America – how about my heart or liver . . . or both?' Fenner was annoyed by the piddling price the bank manager put on his vital organs and the way he turned the screw further by saying 'he wasn't in America'. Fenner glanced upward for support and then began, 'Look, Mr Thickitt.' He paused to think how he would like to be in a position to tell Mr Thickitt to stick it, but continued. 'All my machines and stock, desk, typewriter, everything – wouldn't that cover the thousand pounds?'

Thickitt thought. 'It would indeed,' he said finally. 'But if you went bankrupt how would we recoup our £45,000 already outstanding?'

The fox was cornered, his bushy tail had been singed, and the lair of Fenner's mind lay exposed to the banking hounds poised for the kill.

The sheer gloom of defeat must have shown in his face, for whilst Fenner would have regarded sincerity as a weakness, the bank manager did not – well, he did like dogs. But, to Fenner's amazement, the bank manager agreed to support his proposed three-day jaunt to the exhibition, but only on a day-to-day basis up to five hundred pounds, with Fenner 'checking in' each day by telephone to account his progress and expenses. Fenner accepted with a smile, but hardly before that smile was dry, he was scheming ways and means to cut his costs as far as he could. His mind was racing, cutting back here, re-organizing there. He barely had time to thank Mr Thickitt, and wish his family 'all the very best in the world' as he bowed his way from Mr Thickitt's office. 'Oh,' said Fenner as a parting pleasantry, 'give your dog a pat for me.'

Fenner's stage was almost set – the workers had agreed; the bank manager had agreed; they were all agreed to go to Southampton and make a success of the venture. Now he had to prepare himself for the possible 'death scene' in his personal drama for survival, controlled by his wife and mother-in-law. He had kept the two women in the dark about the exhibition until he had cleared all the other protagonists out of the way, hoping that he could then shame his wife and mother-in-law if they disagreed with his arrangements, by telling them of the others' agreement. He armed himself for the attack on them; highly explosive perfume for his wife, and flowers of surrender for her mother, and in reserve he took a fully loaded two-pound box of their favourite chocolates. He arrived home and assembled his gifts for the 'happy' landing. His own personal 'D Day' had arrived. He paused at his front door for a momentary prayer, and went in.

'What a wonderful idea,' chorused his wife and mother-in-law almost in unison.

'Good business sense, my boy,' said the elder.

'I'm quite proud of you, Harold,' said the younger.

Shocked by the women's reactions, Fenner thought it must have been the effect of the gifts. He had completely overlooked that his plan, or at least Bootle's invitation to the Exhibition, *was* a good business move. Quickly he allowed the women to believe it was all his idea. Even quicker, and whilst everything seemed to be on a high, he darted in with, 'I don't suppose you'd help with the finance?'

'No,' the two women chorused immediately and firmly.

'Oh,' said Fenner trying to retain the high. 'It doesn't matter really – everything's taken care of.'

'Yes?' said his wife curiously. 'How did you manage all that?'

'Have a bramble-jelly surprise,' he offered, almost forcing the sticky chocolate into her inquiring mouth. 'You'll like this.'

'Where did you get your expenses from?' said his mother-in-law, equally curiously.

'Smell this carnation,' he said, blocking the two inhaling apertures in his mother-in-law's nose with the flower. 'Fit for a queen.' Who, he thought, if I'm not careful, will sniff out more than the flower's scent.

Several more questions from the women made some hairline cracks in Fenner's dam. Here I go again, he thought as he fought back, pleasantly of course. He felt the chocolates were melting and the flower's scent waning as the women pursued him with questions. Cut, retrieve; cut, retrieve; his battle hovered; he needed a big gun; then quickly he fired, 'Fenner Fashions International', at his mother-in-law. 'Lady Fenner – for services to Great Britain?' he broadsided to his wife, then waited.

'I'll have another chocolate dear,' said his wife, practising a curtsy.

'Flowers are so nice at this time of the year,' said his mother-in-law, fingering the *Financial Times* on her lap.

Fenner's mind boomed, VICTORY. He had won, over all adversity; they had all fallen before him, Paddy and the girls, the bank manager, and now his wife and mother-in-law. He had won the battle, now it was just a simple task of collecting all the spoils – monetary spoils.

CHAPTER TWO

'We are not riding in that,' said Paddy adamantly, as Fenner stood with the girls at the rear end of a large removal van parked in the road outside the factory. On instructions from Fenner, the girls had orders to report to the factory as usual, where they would board the 'transport' to take them to Southampton. The girls, assuming the 'transport' would be a coach, had arrived in their best 'going on holiday' clothes; large hats, dresses, trouser suits, and carrying a motley collection of suitcases, shoulder bags, model boxes and carrier bags marked Tesco. In addition to their luggage, they carried items of personal comfort. Olive hugged an awkward looking deck chair that kept falling open. Paddy had brought her rolled electric blanket with cable trailing. Kathy carried a beach wind-shield and a half-inflated lilo that smelled strongly of Ambre Solaire – though stale, one could still detect its aroma. Jo-Jo, in a brightly coloured trouser suit that screamed at one, hid several carrier bags under a huge sombrero, and held a long gaudy coloured beach umbrella like a jousting lance. Lynn had no extras; all she needed seemed to have been neatly packed into a five-piece matched set of imitation lizard-skin suitcases, all labelled *With care – stow away from boilers.*

Fenner had stood in amazement as each one had arrived with their 'accoutrements' and mentally noted a query: whether or not the furniture van was going to be big enough to get everything in it. The arrival of Mabel capped it all, for under her arm nestled a small white, blue-bowed poodle. 'I just couldn't leave Twinky,' she explained.

Fenner had nearly passed quietly into his next life at the very sight of a dog in his party. 'What's the matter with it?' he finally asked, in reply to Paddy's statement about the van.

'We're not going hop picking you know,' stormed Paddy. 'I reckon you've got a bloody cheek, if you expect us ladies to ride all that way in this.'

'I couldn't afford to have a coach and a van. I've had to load in all the machines because they wouldn't take them on a coach.'

'We don't care,' said Paddy, sitting down on a nearby suitcase. 'We're people, not cargo, and as such we want seats.'

'You've got seats,' hastened Fenner. 'You've all got your own work seats in the back there. It's like home from home.'

'Blimey,' said Kathy. 'They're hard enough on our bums all day in the factory. God knows what they'll be like all the way to Southampton.'

'I could never climb up there,' added Olive.

'And nor could I in this skirt,' said Paddy. 'Girls, girls,' pleaded Fenner. 'Look, Tony's made it very comfortable for you all.' He looked round for Tony to support him but Tony was strangely absent. 'Look,' he continued, 'it's not far . . . and we'll be stopping for lunch.'

'It's *dinner* in a transport café,' corrected Kathy, to Fenner's annoyance.

'Well we haven't got time to mess about or we'll never get there.'

'I think we need to renew the transport rate,' said Paddy at last.

'How do you mean?' asked Fenner, feeling the pinch of strained expenses lightening.

'We want a hardship allowance,' demanded Paddy.

'Yes,' said Jo-Jo. 'Sheep travel in more comfort.'

'Why don't you report him to the RSTCP Paddy?' said Olive without thinking.

'I ought to,' thought Paddy aloud. 'This van looks as though it needs disinfecting . . . no, what we want is more stops than just one . . . we want factory stops, just like we have normally.'

'Blimey,' breathed Fenner. 'In that case we won't be moving at all.'

'Well it's either that . . . or we're going home, Mr Fenner.'

Some of the girls looked very disappointed at Paddy's demand and looked to Fenner for his assent. Fenner muttered an evil curse under his breath but finally agreed. He reasoned that if his curse came true, he'd be in the same vehicle as the girls. The girls loaded themselves on board and the van took a distinct dip at the back. Fenner tried to supervise but could not make himself heard above the giggling and chattering of the girls and the constant yapping of Mabel's poodle. He gave up finally and moved to the driving cab, where he climbed in alongside Tony who sat in the driving seat. 'Oh, so this is where you've been hiding?' said Fenner, angrily.

'I didn't want to interfere with the negotiations between workers and management,' he said, reaching out of the window to adjust a driving mirror.

'A little support is not interfering, Tony,' Fenner said sarcastically. 'I've got to work out a new stopping plan now, I shall have to pick the cafés out as I come to them, we haven't got a lot of money you know – I can't afford three-course places.'

'Well they won't let parties in for just one course, Mr Fenner,' said Tony trying to be realistic.

'All right,' said Fenner. '*Two* courses.' Thinking, tea one course, biscuits second course.

They had driven all of three hundred and fifty metres, when there was a knocking on the slide panel behind Fenner's head. He slid it back to reveal Paddy's face framed in the aperture. 'You'll have to stop . . . Olive's been sick.'

'Oh no,' wept Fenner. 'Not on the materials I hope?' ignoring Olive's plight. 'Why couldn't she be sick further on – it's no parking here.' He pointed at a double yellow line.

'I don't care,' said Paddy. 'She can't travel with her back to the engine.'

'We're not a corridor train you know,' retorted Fenner, thinking that if he were caught transporting passengers like this, the police might take a dim view, and a judge might take a bright twenty-pound note.

The first hints of countryside appeared as the van ground its way onward. Houses became more sparse, and the tinges of green dotted the gaps as trees, hedgerows and grass began to replace the boredom of endless bricks. The girls in the van sat precariously on their seats, balancing against the tilts and bumps of the tall lorry. Olive's green face had reddened slightly as the conversation took her mind off the sickly lurches of the van's movement.

'Couldn't we play a game?' said Lynn fidgeting.

'We could if my boyfriend was here,' chirped Kathy.

'How about I-Spy?' said Mabel, steadying the snoozing poodle.

'I can't spell,' groaned Olive, quietly.

'We used to play a game,' said Jo-Jo. 'It's called Can You Go?'

'I don't know about you lot, but I could,' said Paddy, trying to look at her watch under the dim ceiling light. 'How long have we been going?'

'All your life, if you're normal,' said Kathy.

'No,' said Paddy, feeling a greater need. 'Isn't it about time we had a stop?'

'We only stopped ten minutes ago when Lynn spilled that lemonade on Fenner's case,' said Jo-Jo. They looked at the case which seemed to be frothing.

'He wasn't very pleased then, was he?' Kathy commented as she peeled a piece off Fenner's case which had risen in a curl. '*I* think it's cardboard,' she continued as the tiny curl became a long strip, leaving the brown case with a distinct mark running across it.

'I'll give him a bang,' said Paddy, swaying her way to the small panel which slid back in the driving-cab partition. 'I can't wait much longer.'

'There's no "Ladies" here,' said Fenner, screwing his head round far enough to face Paddy at the panel behind his head. 'It's open land.'

'Aren't there any trees?' she asked desperately.

Fenner turned to look. 'How many trees?' he said, turning back to Paddy.

'Look, Mr Fenner, I'm not fixing a rate for trees, but some of us have got to go and go bad.'

Fenner grumbled on.

'We don't have to ask you at the factory every time we want to go.'

Fenner grumbled on.

'Right,' said Paddy. 'We'll form a screen with all this material and go there.' She slammed the panel shut.

As though on elastic, the panel flew back again. 'All right, all right,' said Fenner hastily.

'There's a couple of trees there, Mr Fenner,' said Tony pointing ahead.

'What sort of trees?' asked Fenner impatiently, with one eye on Paddy.

'Silver birch, I think.'

'I don't mean that,' screamed Fenner. 'Are they thick or thin? Can the girls go behind?' he said again without turning to look.

'Oh yes,' said Tony. 'I'll pull over, though it's on a bend.'

'Doesn't matter. Let's get it over with.'

Tony pulled the van into the side of the road and parked. Fenner got out to open the back doors and as he did, an urgent mass of femininity poured out past him, excitedly chattering, and made their way to the small clump of trees just off the roadside. Fenner turned his back on them and cringed at such remarks as, 'Mind that, there's a cow been there,' from Mabel who thought it all revolting and firmly told her poodle so.

'I hope there's no stinging nettles,' said Jo-Jo.

'Here, the grass is all wet,' said Olive finding a damp patch with her foot. 'That's what my boyfriend said the other week – but I didn't care.'

Approaching the parked van on the opposite side of the road came a large tractor, towing a rather wide, spraying implement behind. As the following traffic behind the tractor saw the van parked, they were unable to overtake and so formed an impatient queue behind the slow moving tractor. Meanwhile, seeing the road blocked by the half-parked van and the oncoming tractor, a long line of assorted vehicles were forced to stop behind the van, waiting for the road to clear. Fenner stood near the van in embarrassment, quietly cursing the girls. The tractor drew level with the van and as it slowly passed Fenner, the driver gave him a friendly wave, as is the custom of country people. Fenner smiled at this civil gesture, but his smile soon vanished at the other, not so friendly gestures and remarks from the following drivers. He prayed that the ground would open up and swallow him as the insults were joined by the annoyed hooting from the vehicles in the queue behind the van. As the girls emerged from behind the trees, the insults and hootings were now orchestrated by the cat-calls and whistles. Several of the girls giggled, Lynn blushed, and Olive said, 'What's happening?'

'You did it on purpose,' Paddy accused Fenner as she and the others climbed aboard the van.

Fenner stood alone after closing the doors behind them and surveyed quickly what had once been a quiet part of a country road, but was now a seething chaos of noise and vehicles with him at the centre, more reminiscent of the V-Day parade celebrating the end of World War II. He raced to the cab and got into the van, urging Tony to make a rocket assisted take-off to prevent World War III starting, with him as the cause.

Others were converging on Southampton, for cruising up the Solent towards the river Hamble was the huge twin-screwed diesel yacht *Checkmate.* Its sleek lines allowed it to glide through the choppy seas, the white-painted hull reflected in the water, giving the whole picture the look of a shimmering gown suspended by the waves. At the wheel the captain saw Calshot point to his port side and knew the entrance to Hamble river lay not far ahead of his starboard bow. Resplendent in his finery, Sheikh Ali Achmud reclined in his easy chair beneath a sun awning stretched across the afterdeck. Around him sat a bevy of beauties that would grace any film set, the sheikh's harem were chosen for their beauty as well as their more obvious charms. In the warm sun, they attended his every need, but his gaze lay on another beauty – Fawley oil refinery, opposite the entrance to Hamble river. Hamble was ideally convenient for the sheikh, for it would be from his yacht that he could easily visit the ultimate destination of his black gold, the refinery in which he had such an interest, and the reason for his wealth – OIL. The captain sounded the required blasts on the ship's hooter and turned slowly to starboard, lining up *Checkmate* for the middle ground approach to the river Hamble. The craft passed hundreds of small craft moored either side of the central channel. The furthest from the 'Ditty Box' as the central quay was called, the cheaper the mooring fees. Not so with *Checkmate* – she would have the prize berth, befitting the sheikh's wealth and position, for he was not only welcome in Hamble by those who would carry out several maintenance jobs on *Checkmate* but by none other than the British Government, who also welcomed the sheikh – and his oil – to Southampton.

At about the same time the sheikh's yacht tied up to the most expensive berth in Hamble, so Fenner Fashions' removal lorry turned into Mike's Transport Café. The girls in the back could tell that they were stopping, and as it was their official lunch-break they all assumed rightly that they were stopping for lunch. However, never in their wildest dreams did they expect such a dirty broken-down café as that which greeted their eyes as Tony opened the doors for them to 'disembark'. Had it not been for Olive's 'urgency' for a stop, Paddy would have instructed the girls to stay put. Fenner, who had gone ahead of them to make 'arrangements', was lucky to be out of earshot of the words that the girls uttered, concerning his meanness and penny pinching on such bare necessities as food. Paddy set her eye firmly on the café entrance and ordered the girls to, 'Follow me.'

The pungent smell of stale cooking glued itself to the girls' nostrils as they entered. The unswept floor supported several tables and chairs, at which three or four men sat in various stages of eating. The uncollected plates at most of the free seats were either signs that the café had recently been filled to capacity or the plates just hadn't been collected. This proved to be the case, as Paddy found when seating herself at an empty table. She attempted to push away the used plate in front of her, but it had stuck to the table. Paddy looked around for Fenner as the other girls took seats at the table, joined by Tony. 'I bet Fenner never thought he'd end his days in Mike's Transport Café,' said Paddy as she stalked her prey with panther-like eyes.

'Blimey,' said Kathy. 'The Greasy Spoon near the factory is better than this.'

'And it's been closed twice by the health inspector,' added Olive who suddenly didn't find her 'urgency' urgent.

'If he thinks he's going to settle for this sort of thing all through this trip, we're all going home now,' said Paddy, her fire of anger smouldering. 'We are not going another yard until I get a few things straight.'

Fenner finally came out from a back room of the café with the proprietor – plump, unshaven, in his fifties, and dressed in jeans and a dirty singlet upon which weeks of ash had fallen from the smouldering cigarette hanging from one corner of his mouth. Fenner crossed to the seated girls and spoke to Paddy. 'Well, I have arranged the menu with the chef, and he'll soon have our lunches ready – would you all like tea to start . . . I always think a nice cup . . .'

'We're not stopping,' said Paddy in a tone that suggested she might use a meat cleaver on Fenner.

He sensed this right away and could only muster a weak, 'Why, whatever's the matter?'

'*You* are the matter,' said Paddy, rising menacingly. 'This pig's swillbin excuse for a café is the matter. In fact this whole bloody trip is the matter, and my girls are not moving until a few things have been sorted out.' Paddy thumped the table, making sauce bottles rattle on the other tables too, and sat down defiantly.

'Look, girls,' said Fenner, appealing to the group. 'You wanted to stop at factory times and this place happened to be right here at your normal lunchtime, so here we are.'

'Seems all right to me,' said Tony, looking around him. It took some time for the pain to register on Tony's face after his shin had been dented under the table by a pointed woman's shoe. 'What's that for?' he said painfully. The culprit wouldn't answer, but he got the feeling that there would be another kick on the way if he said any more.

'We'll drive on to a better place,' said Paddy, receiving nods from the girls.

'Yes,' said Kathy, scratching. 'I'm beginning to itch.'

'That smell's making me sick again,' said Olive, turning olive.

'Look at this grease,' said Mabel, dabbing her fingers on the table and holding them up for view.

'It's more like a garage than a café,' said Lynn.

'Oh, you'll feel better when we've all had a cup of tea,' said Fenner, gesturing to the owner that they were ready.

'We are not stopping here a minute longer,' said Paddy. 'The trip's off, we're going home.'

'But . . .' began Fenner only to be interrupted by the proprietor, fag waggling in his mouth. 'I'm sorry, madam,' he said to Mabel. 'Dogs are not allowed in 'ere.'

The girls looked at the man in horror.

'You're right,' said Mabel. 'This dog's *too* clean for this place.'

'I don't suppose it would eat here in any case,' said Kathy.

'Right, and nor are we,' said Lynn, surprising all with her forthrightness.

'Now wait a minute,' said Fenner. 'You wanted to stop for lunch at factory times, so here we are.'

Paddy rose from her seat, reaching for her handbag. 'Is there a telephone here?' she asked the proprietor.

'It's over there on the wall,' he answered, thumbing the direction.

'Very well,' said Paddy to Fenner and the proprietor. 'I am now going to phone the health inspector, the *Daily Mirror* and our Union head office, in that order.' Then she pushed past Fenner to the phone.

'Now Paddy look . . .' Fenner reasoned, following her and feeling that Fenner Fashions might crumble in a blaze of publicity. He could see it now: *Fenner girls and Health Minister take action.*

'We can work out something . . . I mean.' Paddy began to pick up the telephone. 'Look, wait a minute . . . what is it you want?'

Paddy paused: 'We want a meal – a proper meal – in a clean place, that's all . . . for the time being.'

There was a clink of plates and cutlery from the girls' table that attracted their attention. The girls had started to clear their table of dirty dishes, placing them on the counter and, taking a cloth from around the proprietor's waist, had begun to wipe the table.

' 'Ere, what's going on?' he protested.

'We'll do it ourselves,' said Kathy, pushing him out of the way.

'Oi, this is my café,' he pleaded as the girls got busy.

'It won't be when the health inspector gets here,' said Jo-Jo, heading for the kitchen.

'Can't you stop 'em?' appealed the proprietor to Fenner who was standing mouth open, watching the girls' activity.

'My girls have given me an idea,' said Paddy, leaving Fenner holding the unplaced telephone receiver. 'One word out of you,' she said to the owner, 'and we'll close you down, now 'op it.'

Jo-Jo was joined by Paddy in the kitchen.

'What have they got to eat here?' said Paddy, opening the fridge. 'Ah, this is more like it,' and she took out a box of steaks.

'Here's some mushrooms,' volunteered Jo-Jo from half inside a cupboard.

'And we've got eggs here as well,' said Paddy. 'Right, so it's steak, eggs, chips and mushrooms – get Olive, she can cook.'

Olive entered and was given instructions by the new

'manageress', who then left to supervise the others. 'Get a broom and sweep up,' she ordered the proprietor, who meekly obeyed. 'And you,' she said to Fenner, 'sit down there in this chair, and if you say one word, I'm on that phone.' She pointed to the instrument of his possible destruction.

The speed at which the 'staff' of Mike's Transport Café moved was staggering to say the least. Paddy had organized the 'shop floor' and everything was like a well-oiled clock that ticked industriously.

'I wish you worked like this in the factory,' sighed Fenner. Some of the diners who had been in the café when Fenner and the girls had arrived, realized that if they stayed they could very easily be put to work – seriously put to work – so to a man, they upped and awayed as fast as their bulging boiler suits would allow. Soon the meals started to emerge from the kitchen. Fenner looked aghast.

'I arranged for egg and chips for everybody,' he shouted above the bustle.

'Well,' said Kathy, now sporting a waitress's apron, 'you ordered it and that's what *you've* got.' She put in front of him a few chips huddling together on the plate next to a small lonely egg.

'Here,' protested Fenner. 'You've all got steaks.'

Fenner glared at Tony beside him and watched as he surgically cut his steak into small segments, mounting each in turn with a portion of mushroom and chip, speared them with his fork and then, dipping the small kebab into the egg yolk, drew it into his mouth with great savour.

Tony looked back at Fenner who was searching through his meal for edible pieces like an old tramp in the dustbins of Soho or New York. 'Want a dip in my egg?' he offered, feeling sorry for Fenner.

'No,' snapped Fenner.

'Please yourself,' said Tony not feeling sorry for him.

''Ere,' said Kathy to Paddy, who was now relieving Olive in the kitchen, 'there's six smashing-looking lorry drivers just arrived and they think I'm a waitress.'

'What makes 'em think that?' was the reply as Paddy turned a sizzling steak in the pan.

'Well one of 'em's just pinched my bum.'

'Saucy blighters, I'd put it on their bill for two pins.'

'Well you can,' giggled Kathy. 'They've just ordered steak, egg and chips all round.'

'Well, don't just stand there. Go and set their table while I cook it.'

Kathy left with an excited squeal. Fenner looked at his watch, dinner hour today had been doubled. He was annoyed, but what was annoying him further was that the girls and the lorry drivers were now dancing all around the café, to the pop music from a transistor radio, and everybody bar him had been well fed and was enjoying themselves, whilst the vision of his fight for survival became blurred with the heavy cigarette smoke that filled the café.

'The last time I danced,' said Mabel to her burly partner, 'was at the ladies' bowling club V-Day dance.'

' 'Ere!' said Lynn to the tall dark handsome stranger who caressed her. 'Funny thing, my mum said dancing like this is not nice – wonder where she got that from?'

'Are you sure this dance is called the screw?' said Jo-Jo twirling with her dance 'instructor'. 'I thought it was called the twist.'

'What would your boyfriend say if he could see you now?' called Paddy to Kathy who had discarded her apron and undone a daring amount of blouse buttons, revealing more of her ample bosom.

'It's not so much what he'd say than what he'd want to do,' said Olive as Kathy bounced to the dance.

Suddenly, off went the music, catching the dancers in various poses of wild dancing.

'You'll get me arrested,' said a nervous proprietor. 'I ain't got a dancing licence 'ere.'

'No,' said Paddy collecting her handbag, 'and you shouldn't have a food licence either . . . come on girls.'

The girls collected their things and made for the door.

'Quick,' Fenner ordered Tony, 'go and get them in the van.'

Tony rose reluctantly, saying, 'Nice party wasn't it?' as he left.

'Go on,' urged Fenner as the last of his party left.

The lorry drivers left too, chatting up the birds as they went, and the café, heavy-hung with smoke and smelling of edible food looked bare and empty.

'I've got your bill 'ere mate,' said the proprietor advancing with a grubby sheet of paper. 'They've eaten me out of house and home.'

'Twenty-one quid?' screamed Fenner, reading the bill. 'You told me you'd do it cheap.'

'Well,' came the reply, 'you would invite six lorry drivers as well, what can you expect?'

'I didn't invite those bloody drivers,' sobbed Fenner.

'Oh! It must have been one of your party.'

'Yes,' said Fenner, paying the bill. 'And I know which one it was.'

The proprietor took the money and counted it again. 'Don't I get a tip?' he said, looking at a departing Fenner.

'Yes, I'll give you a tip . . . if you go to Manchester, take an umbrella.' So saying, Fenner stormed out slamming the greasy door.

The van trundled on to Southampton, passing through several small towns and villages along the way. Fenner sat in silence trying to work out how many times they had stopped and if they had exceeded the normal factory breaks. He quietly worked out in his head that those amount of stops at the factory would constitute a 73-hour day, and they weren't even at their destination yet. Olive had been sick again and Mabel's poodle had to have a run, which it did, and then back in the van it promptly peed against a roll of material. The girls laughed hysterically when Fenner was forced to stop and 'go' himself. He couldn't imagine how thick Paddy's union rule book must be to include all the regulations she quoted at him concerning stopping, tea breaks, leg-stretching time, plus hardship money for the mode of travel. He didn't really dislike Paddy; she was a good worker and a capable girl really, but, 'Too bloody red!' he muttered to himself. Pity, he thought, I could have fancied her. He continued to think about the other girls in his employ – they weren't a bad lot really. Olive was a bit dim, but then someone had to be. Jo-Jo – she had settled well in the factory as she had done in England, though she could work a bit faster, he thought. Kathy was too interested in her boyfriend to concentrate on speedy work – he'd have to watch her, and it wasn't difficult really – she did have a good figure. Lynn and Mabel were his youngest and eldest. He liked them – they were quieter types of girls and worked well. Too much chatter meant less concentration and work production. He had installed a radio in the workroom so they couldn't hear themselves talk, but now they just shouted. He looked across at Tony. With a bit more polishing he could come into management, thought Fenner. It would have been nice to have a son to carry on and run the business. Still, never mind, babies were expensive, especially if his wife had one. He winced at what she'd spend in Mothercare. No, he'd settle for Tony, he was cheaper. Had he married Paddy for instance, she'd probably like kids – she could tell them what to do. Yes, she'd be good at that. Really, Paddy and his wife were very much alike, he thought – he thought again – yes, they were – they both nagged him . . . they were the same all right. The panel behind Fenner slid back with a bang.

'Ain't it about time we were there?' called Paddy.

Fenner awoke with a start at the sound. 'What's happened?' he said, with a yawn.

'Paddy wants to know if we're there yet,' said Tony.

'Well, you're the one that's driving – are we?'

Tony looked around him and then saw a milestone which said Southampton 5 miles. He reported to Fenner and Paddy.

'On a milestone!' said Paddy. 'They were for stagecoaches not lorries.'

'What's the difference? It's the same mileage then and now.'

'No, it's not,' insisted Paddy. 'It's metres now and they're longer.'

'Trust you to know the difference,' said Fenner. 'Anyway, metres or miles, we're nearly there, so tell the girls to get ready.'

'Coo,' said Paddy. 'I can't wait to soak in the bath at the hotel.'

'The bathroom may be engaged,' suggested Tony.

'Don't be silly. Every room has a bathroom now.' Fenner lowered himself in his seat trying to be inconspicuous.

The removal van pulled up outside the Polygon Hotel, a top class hotel in Southampton that Fenner had directed Tony to drive to and park.

'Shan't be a tick,' said Fenner and he climbed out of the cab and went into the hotel. Tony got out too, stretched his legs and walked to the back of the van and let out all the girls.

'Ooh, this is nice,' said Kathy, looking at the hotel.

'Yes,' said Paddy, 'I demanded a good hotel.' The others got out, admired the hotel and trouped into the foyer. The large carpeted foyer indicated the luxury of the building, especially when a porter came across and inquired about their luggage.

'Oh, it's all outside,' said Paddy. 'There's quite a lot.'

'Very good, madam. I'll get a couple of other porters.'

'Where's Fenner?' said Jo-Jo.

'Doing the reservations,' said Mabel.

'Ooh look, pictures of the hotel,' said Lynn. 'I'll send my mum one, she'll be pleased I'm at a good hotel.' She scribbled on the card, stamped it and dropped it into the hotel postbox. Whilst Lynn was writing, the three astonished porters unloaded the girls' luggage from the van.

'Cor blimey,' said one, 'how much more?'

'Quite a bit yet,' said a porter's voice, deep in the darkness of the van's innards. 'Do they want all these sewing machines as well, do you reckon?'

'Christ I hope not – let's just take the cases first.'

'They must be with a theatre group, Gilbert and Sullivan I should think,' said a porter in the dark.

'No, they're birds – more likely a strip show,' said another.

'Cor,' said the third.

'What are you all doing out of the van?' said Fenner, appearing at last.

'We want to get to our rooms,' said Paddy. 'I want my bath.'

'Well, all back in the lorry. This hotel's full.' Fenner strode towards the exit.

'Oh, what a right muckup,' said Olive, collecting her things.

'I thought it was too good to be true,' said Kathy.

'Me too,' agreed Mabel.

'That bloody man,' said Paddy. 'I bet he hasn't booked *anywhere* in advance.'

'Oh dear,' said Lynn following Paddy and the others through the exit. 'I've just sent my mum a card where I'm staying.'

'Never mind,' said Mabel, 'she'll like the thought.'

'Well you'll just have to put it all back again,' Fenner was saying to the three tired porters.

'Mr Fenner,' said Paddy looking aggressive. 'I want a word with you.'

'And so do I, sir,' said a large policeman. 'You'll have to move this van from here.'

That's a Godsend, thought Fenner at the arrival of the policeman – he wouldn't have to answer Paddy's questions. 'Yes, officer, of course,' said Fenner politely. 'We're just going, sir.'

'What a crawler he is,' said Kathy as they all clambered aboard again.

Tony shut the doors and climbed in the cab. Fenner began to get in when a hotel porter tapped him on the shoulder and just stood there awaiting a tip. Fenner was about to ignore him, when he spied the policeman reaching for his notebook, so he quickly produced a pound note and gave it to the porter.

'There's three of us, sir,' said the porter.

Trapped, thought Fenner. 'Bloody well trapped and conned for three quid,' said Fenner to Tony as they drove away. 'And we're not even staying there.'

'Didn't you book in advance?' said an irate Paddy from the slide panel.

'I thought there'd be plenty of rooms,' pleaded Fenner.

'What, with an exhibition going on in the town! We'd better be at a good hotel,' she warned and slammed the panel shut to prove she meant it.

They tried several more hotels, Fenner going in alone and reappearing to announce, 'Full up.' Each hotel they called at was getting less glamorous than the last. The girls would never know that Fenner was bribing the reception staff to say they were full up, for in that way it would be cheaper than staying at the hotels they visited. Fenner realized he couldn't keep saying the hotels were full, so he introduced more excuses, each visit a different one and each hotel getting more dowdy.

'They won't take dogs,' he reported through the panel at one place. 'Three in a bed,' he said at another.

The girls, ignorant of Fenner's bribing activities, tolerated it for some time, though they were getting agitated all the time. Fenner's excuses were wearing thin now, and when he said, 'Dormitory sleeping only,' Paddy intervened.

'We're stopping at the next hotel, whatever it costs,' she said through the sliding panel. 'We're all fed up with this stopping and starting. Olive's been sick again and it's made Mabel's poodle sick now.'

Fenner didn't mind at all now they had worked their way from the city centre and were in the docks area of Southampton, where any hotel looked cheap. The lorry stopped once more and as Fenner got out, Paddy called from the back of the lorry, 'And it better not be a temperance hotel either.'

Fenner sneered and went into a very seedy looking place. Shortly after, he came out and announced to the tired travellers that the hotel could accommodate everybody. Gratefully, the weary girls climbed out of the van and looked at the hotel. It was a large, three-storeyed terraced house; over the central doorway entrance hung a sign slightly tilted to one side which read Lighthouse Hotel. It all looked very dowdy indeed, with peeling paint and dark foreboding curtains at the windows. Above the doorway, suspended on a bracket, hung a small replica of a lighthouse, that swung squeakily to and fro in the light breeze.

'Call this a good hotel?' asked Paddy.

Fenner turned. 'Look, the town's full, we're lucky to get in anywhere; at least they can take us all.'

It made sense really, and as Paddy looked at the others, she could tell that they were so exhausted from the long journey they didn't care where they stayed. 'OK,' she said finally. 'It'll do for one night at least.' In a party, they trouped into the hotel foyer, well, rather more a passage, with a hatchway in the wall over which hung a sign that read, *Reception, please ring.* Fenner rung the bell which none of them could hear, but someone must have because the hatch flew up and a very tartily made-up lady showed herself in the opening. Recognizing Fenner from his original inquiries, she greeted the ladies with, 'Oh hello, ducks. You have had a long journey haven't you? I'll show you your rooms.' With that, she dropped the hatch down and a few seconds later reappeared in the passage. Normally such a place would have driven Paddy and the girls into the street, but the tiring journey and the landlady's pleasant greeting relaxed them enough to accept the tatty accommodation almost without a murmur. Mustering all their strength, they managed to climb to the top floor of the building to see their rooms. It had been carpeted most of the way, as their rooms were, with what must have been good carpet years ago, but which now had worn into odd pieces of pile held together with tattered threads. The wallpaper was also worn brown with age and was peeling at many points. The landlady puffed it to the second floor then directed them on alone to the top which the girls, Fenner and Tony finally attained in a near state of collapse.

'Christ,' puffed Paddy. 'Now I know how Tensing must have felt on Everest.' As she was the first to reach the 'summit', she looked back down the 'mountain' at the rest of the struggling climbers. They were all helping each other, to such a degree that stronger bonds were growing between members of the party, as they battled for the top.

'Are you sure this place is the only one with rooms to spare?' Paddy asked Fenner as she sat on the top landing. Fenner didn't answer – he needed all of his valuable breath to save his own life, and not waste it on answering stupid questions.

'We wouldn't have got these if it hadn't been for a cancellation,' called Lynn from a ledge further down as she saved Olive from collapse.

'I think I'd rather have slept in the van,' said Kathy, joining Paddy on the peak.

Fenner's eyes lit with the suggestion but he was unable to comment, he cursed his spent lungs for making him miss such a valuable saving. The remainder of the party were finally pulled on to the top landing and stood gently breathing, for too much 'in' breath may well have resulted in burst lungs.

'I can't get my breath,' gasped Jo-Jo. 'Don't worry,' said Paddy, with a sneer at Fenner, 'it's the high altitude.'

There were three rooms off the landing and the girls opened them and inspected them in turn. One was a large room, tattily decorated in the same decor as the landing and stairs – 'worn and grotty'. There were two large old-fashioned double beds with brass ends, a wardrobe and dressing-table. Kathy opened the wardrobe door and with the weight of a large full length mirror on the inside of the door, and the leaning floor, the empty wardrobe creaked and began to topple forward towards Kathy, who was saved from being crushed under the Victorian monster by the prompt action of Tony. Having regained their breath, the girls' conversation began to grow.

'Well caught,' jibed Paddy. 'It would have flattened her.'

'Your boyfriend wouldn't have been very pleased,' noted Jo-Jo, nodding towards Kathy's ample bosom.

'They might have saved me,' said Kathy in defence.

They trooped to the next room which was smaller than the first and contained a double and a small double bed. The wardrobe was single size and the dressing-table the same. Unfortunately, the slope of the roof reflected itself in the ceiling and to get to the dressing-table or into the double bed necessitated a distinct lean to the left or right, according to whether one was going to bed, or getting out of it.

'I've never seen a sloping ceiling before,' said Olive, crouching under it.

'Well we don't usually sleep in attics,' said Paddy for Fenner's benefit, who had now regained his breath and colour. 'It's only for a few nights and besides there's nowhere else for us.'

Mabel who had gone to the dressing-table, tried to open the drawer. It wouldn't move. 'Why won't it open? What's stopping it?'

'It's the woodworms holding hands,' joked Kathy as the party moved to the third room.

On the landing outside the door was a cupboard and on its door was written in chalk *Wardrobe for this room*. Underneath was an arrow pointing to the door. Tony opened the door, which stuck half-way. He led the way in as the others filed in behind. The room was all bed – a large double bed left only a small gap between it and the wall. They stood in a line looking at it.

'This must be your room,' said Paddy to Fenner.

'Well,' he answered, 'it's small but I'll be all right in here.'

'Of course you will. You'll have Tony to keep you company.'

Fenner tried to turn to speak to Paddy but only his head had room to and that at a tilt against the sloping ceiling. 'Now, wait a minute, I usually sleep alone,' he said in protest.

'Well all that's at an end now,' said Paddy, side-stepping out of the room. 'Can't we have a room with two beds?' said Tony, looking distastefully at Fenner.

'Normally, yes,' said Paddy, but it's all we've got – everywhere else is full – isn't it Mr Fenner?' she finished, turning the knife.

Out on the landing Paddy 'issued' the rooms to the girls – they were going to have to sleep together in pairs and they looked at each other strangely, trying to pick a bed-mate.

'I like to have Twinky on the bed with me,' announced Mabel.

'OK,' said Paddy looking around. 'Olive,' she said finally, 'you like dogs don't you?'

'No.'

'Good,' said Paddy. 'That's you two settled.'

Whilst she continued with the allocations, Fenner peeked into his 'wardrobe'. Inside the cupboard was a large hot water storage tank with dusty asbestos lagging hanging from it; alongside the tank was one, bent wire coat-hanger. He cringed as he looked at his nice suit jacket and visualized it 'furred' with asbestos flakes.

'As I've got to look after Lynn,' said Paddy to Kathy and Jo-Jo, 'you two can take one double, and we'll take the other in the big room. Olive and Mabel in there.' She pointed to the second bedroom.

The girls looked disgruntled, until Paddy added, 'Don't worry girls, as we're sleeping double, we'll all be on double time whilst we're here.'

Fenner spun round, slamming the cupboard door, spraying the landing with a fine asbestos dust. 'Double time?' he coughed through the mist. 'How do you work that out?' he said to Paddy.

'Simple – two on a job, double time, two in a bed, double time.'

'Where does it say that?'

'Rule 78, section five,' said Paddy confidently. 'If a worker suffers dual hardships in pursuit of his normal working he or she shall be paid at double time rate for the said hardship for the duration of the particular period.'

'Where's the dual hardship?' begged Fenner.

'Two in a bed.'

'That's one,' pleaded Fenner.

'And these bloody stairs,' said Paddy, looking down into the dark chasm of the winding staircase. 'And now if you'll kindly bring up our luggage, we'd like to get settled in.'

And with that, the girls moved to their respective rooms as Twinky yapped approval.

Fenner stood, flabbergasted by the rule Paddy had quoted, and wondered if she'd just made it up, promising himself to investigate it later. He looked at Tony. 'Mine's the brown case with HF on it,' he said and side-stepped into his bedroom.

Paddy, Kathy, Jo-Jo and Lynn were not saying anything to

each other as they inspected their room. Each was silent, alone with their own thoughts. Paddy, though far from happy at the shabby treatment from Fenner, was at least seeing that he had paid for it, and she would find other ways to wrestle Fenner from his money as efficiently as she could. She knew him of old. Lynn sat on the bed and thought she could hear her mother gasp and then faint, after discovering that her little girl was not in the fine hotel on the postcard, but in a dockside 'doss house' and subject to the rigours of an unsavoury stay, not only from seamen, but from every seaman 'across the wide Missouri'. She fell back on the bed in horror and into what seemed to be a hole in the middle of the bed. She lay there, head down, looking up at her feet, like two tiny faces peering down at her.

Kathy, who had been more accustomed to 'hotels' before with her boyfriend than the others, was busily trying to prise open one of the dressing-table's three drawers. After screwing back in the handle of one drawer, she pulled the face off the drawer beneath, leaving just a dark shelf of the remainder of the drawer stuck inside. She pulled out an old newspaper that had been lining the bottom of the drawer and read the yellowing print to herself. *Food Rationing to End*, said the fading headline.

Jo-Jo stood near her bed feeling how far the hole went in her bed, as it had in Lynn's. She groped around, plunging her hands down in different places. It was like feeling the ribs of someone who had been on a hunger strike for about three years. She identified by feel various springs, metal supports, and clumps of knotted mattress with her hands. It reminded her of the hills and slopes of her native land, with a hill each side of a wooded slope and the dried river bed at the bottom. The dried river bed at the bottom of her immediate valley was the floor. She looked across at Kathy's well-proportioned body, which was far more than her own well-covered frame, and visualized them both lying down in their respective places, then cascading down the slopes to the centre of the bed, like great boulders disturbed by the seasonal monsoon rains.

'I don't think I could sleep with a dog,' said Olive, poking her head round the door to Paddy. 'I mean Arthur's hairy but not furry – and he hasn't got a cold nose.' Olive's timid intrusion brought the girls back to reality from their thoughts. 'You see, I don't want to upset Mabel,' Olive went on. 'But she hasn't slept with a man before, only a dog.'

'Then what are you worried about?' questioned Paddy.

'Well . . .' started Olive.

'The worst you'll get is a biscuit then,' chipped in Kathy.

'No, I mean . . . it might lay on me!'

'Yes,' said Jo-Jo. 'I see what you mean.'

She thought of Kathy's bulk rolling down the 'hillside'.

'Can someone help me up?' called Lynn from the hole, wanting to add her comments. Now the girls seemed to have feelings of discontent among themselves which was new to them; normally it was against Fenner, which was easy and sometimes fun. They had no immediate enemy now, a strange situation indeed, and not being sure how to handle it, they turned their tragedies to humour. The laughing had started as Paddy and Kathy heaved on Lynn to pull her out of the dip in the bed. With two of them pulling, Lynn came out easily, whilst Paddy and Kathy bumped into Olive and knocked her into the hole in the next bed.

'Sorry Olive,' chorused the giggling girls, as they grabbed Olive's flailing legs and levered her to her feet.

'I thought the floor had collapsed,' said Olive re-adjusting her spectacles.

'Here,' said Kathy looking at the beds' dips. 'These beds don't half sag in the middle.'

'They must be marriage beds,' said Jo-Jo grinning; the girls squealed with laughter.

'Is your bed like this at home Olive?' said Lynn curiously.

'No, we've got twin beds, Arthur and me.'

'Go on,' said Kathy. 'Who does the quick dash across the gap, you or him?

'Oh, it's not like that,' she said truthfully.

'It is,' butted in Paddy. 'You told me one of your beds was nearly new.'

The girls squealed even more at this banter, so much so that it brought in Mabel from the next room. 'What's all the laughing about?' she asked, clutching Twinky.

'We were laughing about the dip in our beds,' said Jo-Jo.

'Is yours like that?' Kathy asked Mabel.

'Oh, no. Ours is really as stiff as a board.'

'How do you mean?'

'Well I pulled back the mattress and it's all boarded over underneath.'

The girls roared even more when Jo-Jo added, 'Coo, it's really bed and board here isn't it?'

'Talk about being thrown together,' chided Paddy.

'Quite disgusting,' said Mabel, who was totally out of her depth with the situation.

'I hope there's no reds under the bed,' Olive quoted from a phrase she'd heard on radio.

'Why?' said Jo-Jo, winking at Kathy. 'Frightened you're going to get attacked?'

'If they try, they'll need a saw,' said Paddy, falling on to the bed laughing.

Fenner, who had been sitting in his bedroom totting up his dwindling expenses, heard the gaiety and laughter coming from the girls' room, thought it strange that the girls were laughing; he had expected far more wrath from Paddy at the hotel he had chosen. The landlady had gladly accepted the bribe to make the bill even cheaper if the girls shared beds and he took top floor rooms. These were always the hardest to let in view of the absence of a lift, and yes, she had continued, taking a further bribe, 'pie and chips', 'fish and chips' and 'egg and chips', fitted her menu ideally; she would attend to it personally. She would have done in any case, but she thought it sounded helpful and co-operative to say so to Fenner, as he was the one handing out money.

Fenner thought, as the girls were in a happy mood, he would go and outline what needed to be done at the exhibition hall the next day in preparation for the opening to the public. He knocked on the main room door where all the girls were still giggling, and was invited in.

'Ah, girls,' he said. 'I'm glad to see you settling in OK.'

'Oh yes, Mr Fenner,' said Paddy sitting on the bed. 'We were just about to knock off for the day.'

Fenner looked puzzled. 'Knock off?' he questioned. 'Yes. We've had a long day, what with the journey and moving in, so we thought we'd have an early night.'

'Oh yes, of course, good,' said Fenner, thinking the girls meant to turn in early, saving the cost of dinner.

'So we've finished work now, and going down for our tea.'

'Yes,' said Fenner having been foiled as to the girls' meaning. 'You mean moving in was working?'

'Of course. We normally work to five-thirty at the factory,

but as we're staying on the job, we are entitled to a tea break at five, and by the time we've had that it'll be knocking off time at five-thirty.'

'Well said,' said Kathy as she collected her handbag.

Outside the door there was a bumping and banging and suddenly a tired Tony staggered in, carrying several cases. 'I'm just about all in,' he gasped.

'What?' said Paddy. 'Did Mr Fenner get you to carry up all our cases?'

'Well, I carried some of them,' said Tony exhaustedly, 'but the porter helped me.'

'Porter . . . here,' said Fenner. 'I'm not paying for any porter whilst you're still on pay.' As he strode to the door a giant of a man peeked into the room.

'In 'ere?' he said.

'Oh, yes please,' said Tony. The man came in carrying five cases, a deck chair and an umbrella. He was six foot two or three, had arms like a man's thighs, and highly tattooed. He wore jeans and a shirt and looked as though he could carry the luggage, girls and Fenner as well.

'This is the porter,' introduced Tony, 'that you're not going to pay.'

'Oh, well, I meant not pay till he got here,' said a terrified Fenner. He reached into his pocket and pulled out some loose change and kept paying the man till he smiled.

'Thank you, guv,' grunted the man. 'Oh, by the way, grub is . . . er, dinner is served.'

They all descended the stairs, with Paddy and Fenner arguing if this would be late tea or early dinner.

CHAPTER THREE

'Egg and chips . . . I thought we'd be having sheep's eyeballs,' said Basil Thornton. Sheikh Ali Achmud retched and was nearly sick. 'Sorry,' said Basil at the obvious blunder, 'but I thought you chappies liked them.' Basil Thornton, a young civil servant from the Foreign Office had been sent by her Brittanic Majesty's Government to greet the arrival of Sheikh Ali

Achmud, his harem, and his oil, at the docking of his luxury yacht, *Checkmate*, at Hamble. Basil had gone aboard *Checkmate* as the gangplank had been lowered, to offer fraternal greetings to the sheikh from Great Britain. Officialities over, Sheikh Ali Achmud, a young man of thirty-two years, tall and good looking, had invited Basil to dinner aboard his yacht. The sheikh, being of the more modern Arab culture, was quite westernized and enjoyed many things which his elders would have fallen on their knees to Allah at the very thought, and though the sheikh retained the basic ideals of his race, he also enjoyed some of the western ways, and one of these 'ways' were egg and chips, which he found very much to his liking and in his eyes, a great English delicacy.

After Basil's *faux pas* about the sheep's eyes, the conversation settled to a more convivial level among the sumptuous surroundings aboard *Checkmate*. Basil was intrigued at the attention he received from the sheikh's harem girls; one of the old ideals the young sheikh enjoyed. The subservience of the girls to Basil was most pleasant, though a little strange, for he was not what anyone would have called a 'ladies man'; on the contrary, his experience with women was limited to the odd partner at the tennis club dance. The sheikh, on the other hand, had women, good-looking women and girls, literally at his fingertips, to obey his every command and wish without thought of a question – the girls accepted this as the way of life and knew no different.

The sheikh outlined to Basil his planned visits during his stay – a visit to the oil refinery, another to the Hawker Siddeley aeroplane factory, yet another to Vosper Thornycroft naval shipbuilders and repairers. All these visits could well be good for British overseas sales and the sheikh would be afforded every assistance to these ends – he was on a shopping spree and this could be good for England. Basil then suggested a further visit for the sheikh, much more on the lighter side, and something that would appeal to the sheikh's 'ladies' – a visit to the 'Buy British' exhibition in Southampton, where all manner of British goods would be on show, and on sale. The sheikh readily accepted Basil's suggestion, as this sort of visit would be light relief on his heavy industrial schedule. He smiled at Basil for his charming suggestion, and Basil felt he had scored a good point for England in pleasing him, and he could see his department being similarly pleased. That for Basil was always a good step in the ladder of promotion. After this pleasant thought, he really enjoyed his egg and chips, and agreed with the sheikh that indeed they were a tasty English delicacy.

'Egg and chips, you must be joking,' roared Paddy to Fenner, across the dining-room table. 'You're not dragging us all the way from our homes to feed us on egg and chips.'

'And what's wrong with egg and chips?'

'Nothing. If you're going to have a quick snack in Joe's Greasy Spoon café. But we're in a hotel now, and it's our dinner,' protested Paddy pushing her plate away.

The girls, Fenner and Tony were all seated around a large table in the hotel's dining-room, by the bay window overlooking the street. It showed passers-by the Lighthouse Hotel was full, and therefore must be a good place to stay. It was a good job those same passers-by couldn't hear the conversations of the guests that made the hotel look full, for it would have surely shattered their illusions. Paddy's outburst caught the other girls in various poses of eating, and though starving hungry, the voice of 'their' lady of the union demanded immediate reactions from them – stop everything and await consultations. They each eyed a chip that hung suspended on their forks before their mouths, and the tomato sauce which further savoured the morsel which sent streams of mouth-watering tears down their chins. Though the eagerness to eat was gnawing at their stomachs – 'No decision had been reached.'

'We're not eating it,' said Paddy on the girls' behalf.

Fenner looked around the table at the other diners held in suspended animation. 'They were just going to, till you stopped them,' he concluded.

Paddy also looked around the table, and in the eyes of all the girls was a look that created a sense of doubt in her mind.

'Look,' said Fenner finally. 'We did come unannounced. It was good of the woman to get us this.' Paddy looked at the girls, each eye seemed to nod, 'Yes.' Looking down at her own dish, she thought she detected her egg decidedly wink at her invitingly, and the pang in her own stomach nudged her into acceptance. 'All right,' she said at last. 'We'll discuss it further whilst we're eating.'

The snap of jaws on chip was almost unanimous, and not a

word was spoken until the pattern on each plate could be clearly seen.

Smoke from the after-meal cigarettes drifted swiftly in the draught from the bay windows and the dried putty in the frames showed signs of cracking and crumbling in keeping with the rest of the room. The dark papered walls were only broken by the odd patches of damp and a few nautical prints, that depicted the beautiful days of sail, which gave a distinct impression that these fine ships were far better built than the walls upon which they hung. Tony broke the thoughtful silence. 'I thought it was very tasty myself.'

Paddy took up the cudgel. 'Tasty? It was cheap, a con because we were hungry. They always serve it here. You can tell that by the plates.'

'What do you mean?' asked Fenner in defence.

'Well, look at the sparrow in the pattern,' she said, moving her knife and fork to one side for all to see.

'What's wrong with it?' asked Tony, as the others looked at their plates to follow the conversation.

'Well I've never seen a yellow sparrow before, that is dried egg yolk.'

'It could be a canary,' ventured Olive, looking at the pattern on Paddy's plate.

'What, in Battersea Gasworks?'

'Oh,' said Jo-Jo. 'I've got a different pattern on mine.'

'So have I,' added Lynn.

'Of course you have,' said Paddy. 'You don't think a place like this would have matching china.'

'She probably picked it up in a jumble sale,' said Kathy.

'I'll tell you,' Paddy went on, 'it's all cheap and nasty, and you ...' she shot a glare at Fenner, 'have booked us in this dump to save money.'

'Save money?' he contested. 'It's cost me a fortune so far and I haven't even sold one dress yet. It might have been cheaper to ship the whole exhibition to my factory than come down here.'

'Well you can't expect us to give our best efforts, feeding us on egg and chips – you'll just have to expect egg and chips production.'

Fenner thought a while, then said, 'Look, girls, this exhibition means a lot to Fenner Fashions, and I want to make a good impression on the customers and Bootles, with our efforts.'

'Well you can always increase production Mr Fenner.'

'Really?' Fenner's interest was renewed. 'How?'

'Better food makes better dresses,' said Paddy leaning back in her creaking chair.

'That's blackmail!'

'No it's not – it's incentive.' Paddy smiled at a male passer-by who smiled back thinking to himself, that must be a good place to stay – it's full up.

Fenner and Tony made their way to the exhibition hall in the furniture van to deliver and set up the machines on their stand.

It was a large, oblong hall, and along each side were rows of raised wooden stands upon which busy workmen and sales people were completing last-minute preparations. Each stand displayed different wares, ranging from china to shoes and watches to furniture – all were gaily decorated with colourful flags, posters and printed signs that displayed the type of wares on show, and the name of the firm selling them. Fenner and Tony walked along the rows amazed at the bustle. Fenner felt quite proud to be in such esteemed company of retailers; he glowed even more with pride when he arrived at his own stand, whose poster shouted proudly *Fenner Fashions International*. With a tingle running through his body, he read on *Bespoke garments on the spot*. He could even feel the thick roll of bank notes bulging in his pockets at the trade he expected to do. He'd be the first in the rag trade to offer altered garments on the spot. He would make large German women elegant, petite French women even more chic. He could hear himself saying, 'Order now and it will be made and ready in three hours' time.'

At this juncture an ugly thought purveyed his mind: Three hours from my girls? More like three days! I'll have to watch that closely. Enough of that. Just think, after all these foreigners had bought their garments and gone home to their distant lands, there wouldn't be any complaints, it would be too far to travel. His thoughts were going wild. Now if we just tacked on the labels, they would eventually fall off, and the customer wouldn't even know our name. Yes – his face twisted in evil thought – and who'll know?

Fenner and Tony arranged the workroom table and machines behind the main stand. The workroom was curtained off all round, leaving the front stand clear for modelling the dresses and the showing of pinned samples on the static models. This would be Fenner's finest hour, everything was falling into place, he had a good pitch in the exhibition, it was a long way from the tea bar for one thing, and it would be open from nine to nine; for another, he couldn't wait for the next day's opening to start shovelling the money in.

At the hotel, the girls sat in the lounge talking among themselves. The lounge was merely an extension of the dining-room, in that the only difference was that the plates, etc., were cleared from the table in the window bay, and the dining-room was now the lounge. The room's harsh unshaded light lit the street and pavement outside; the thin shabby curtains had not proved wide enough to cover the expanse of the windows of the bay and so, seated round the table, they sat as exposed as on a lighted stage to all the passers-by outside in the street.

' 'Ere, that bloke winked at you, Kathy,' said Jo-Jo, as a man passed the window in the street.

'More likely she winked at him,' jibed Paddy, lighting a cigarette.

'It's not nice to wink at strange men,' said Mabel, and she brushed a kiss curl over Twinky's left eye.

'They're all strange till you wink at 'em,' answered Kathy, checking her own kiss-curl with her hand.

'Arthur used to wink at me,' reminisced Olive, 'when I used to work in our local corner shop.'

'Oh, how romantic,' admired Lynn.

'It wasn't really. It was always windy on that corner, and he used to get things in his eye.'

'Oh,' said Lynn sadly. 'Still he married you, didn't he?'

'Eventually,' said Paddy caustically, blowing cigarette smoke at a snoozing Twinky.

'What time have we got to start in the morning?' inquired Jo-Jo.

'Same time as usual I suppose,' offered Kathy, as she winked at the same male passer-by, who out of the girls' view had met two friends and said, 'They're on the game, let's go in and ask how much.'

'Yes, but now we get taken to work, plus travelling time,' said Paddy, pleased with her victorious bargaining.

'Isn't that the same fella who went past a minute ago?' noted Lynn, leaning to look further out of the window.

'I didn't see him,' said Jo-Jo.

'He seems to be coming in,' said Mabel staring out at the front door.

'Don't they lock the front door?' said Lynn, a little worried.

'Not in hotels,' said Kathy, from experience.

Suddenly the lounge dining-room door opened and in walked three men. The girls looked up. 'Evening, girls,' said the man who had winked at Kathy.

'Evening,' chorused the girls in reply.

The man, in his late thirties, wore jeans and a seaman's jacket over an open-necked shirt. He sported a small beard and moustache, different from his colleagues who were both in their early twenties, clean shaven, but similarly dressed.

'It's a nice evening,' said the bearded man.

'We haven't seen much of it,' said Paddy casually. 'We were busy all afternoon upstairs and we've just had our dinner.'

'Good. So you're all free now?'

'Well, we are, but we're still on pay so to speak.'

The girls all giggled; the presence of the men had really broken the boredom, and as always Paddy was speaking for them all, but the girls didn't mind. Kathy, feeling that she would be helping Paddy out with the conversation said, 'We're doing an exhibition tomorrow.'

The bearded man answered, 'Oh, that's a shame, we'll miss it – our ship sails then.'

The two others just nodded, giving a sheepish smile to the girls generally.

'Oh, never mind,' said Olive. 'We'll do another one just for you when you're home again.'

'Yes,' added Lynn, 'and our boss'll be pleased if you'll tell all the foreigners you meet to come as well.'

'We certainly will,' said the bearded one. 'Do you mind if I have a talk with my mates?'

'No, go ahead,' giggled Jo-Jo. 'We've got all night.'

The girls joined Jo-Jo in giggling and laughing whilst the men went into a huddle.

'I can't wait to get to bed,' said Mabel. 'And I know my little Twinky's the same.'

At last, the bearded man turned and spoke to all the girls. 'You'll have to excuse my mates, they're a bit shy, it's their first time you see.'

'Ah,' chorused the girls sympathetically.

'Well,' said the bearded one to Paddy, taking her for the Madam. 'If you can tell us how much it'll be, I'll have this one,' pointing to Kathy, 'and these two,' pointing to Lynn and Jo-Jo, 'for my two mates, just a short time please.'

The *QE II*'s hooter sounded her departure, but it was hardly heard above the combined screams of the girls in the Lighthouse Hotel. Fenner at the Exhibition, some miles away, turned to Tony: 'Did you speak?' he asked in a strange way.

Tony answered 'No.' Fenner said it was funny, because he'd thought he'd heard something. A drunk in the snug bar of the corner pub suddenly sat up from his alcoholic snooze. 'Wha's 'a marrer?' he asked nobody. The Lighthouse sign swung on its bracket outside the hotel, which was strange, as there was no wind to move it.

Tonight was indeed alive with something. A distant clock somewhere in the city of Southampton chimed and told those who heard that it was three o'clock in the morning. The city lay peacefully asleep, the busy streets were at rest and a ship's hooter was muffled by distance far away in the Solent, and the Lighthouse sign outside the hotel hung still in the cool night air. Everything seemed to be at peace and rest, except for the tortured souls of Fenner Fashions staff, who, half asleep, individually battled, to make the most of their uncomfortable beds. Each alone with their hazy thoughts as they tried to sleep, dozing and waking with monotony. The girls had all attacked Fenner verbally for booking them into this seedy hotel where they had been mistaken for 'Home comforts for Seamen', and only a further promise of an increased hardship bonus had abated their fury, until sheer fatigue of their long, hard day had forced their bodies to rest. Olive turned again on her side of the boarded bed she shared with Mabel, and in so doing caused the boards to creak, like the strained mast of a fully rigged clipper, rounding the Horn. Every bone in her body ached from the constant contact with hard squeaky wood. She woke suddenly to see her husband Arthur lying there with his hair in curlers, then, after the sleepy shock, realized it was Mabel next to her; she groaned another turn, almost in tune with the creaking wood. She wondered what Arthur would have said if he knew she'd been 'picked up' by a sailor; she frowned in her sleep at his answer, then smiled as she thought what he'd have said if she had.

Jo-Jo clung to the side of her 'mountain'; both her and Kathy had rolled into each other at the bottom of the dip in their bed; she had woken with a start, imagining herself being crushed by the rolling 'boulder' of Kathy's ample form smothering her at the bottom of the valley. She had tried to waken Kathy to tell her to resume her place on the opposite 'mountain ledge' of the bed. But Kathy had snored her way across the North Sea to join her boyfriend on his lonely oil rig and heard nothing save the gentle lap of rich living from his overtime. Jo-Jo had given a thought to roll Kathy back up the slope of the bed, but had abandoned the attempt after ripping Kathy's nightie trying to get a good grip for the long haul. She was now plagued with worry as to what Kathy might think, seeing her nightdress ripped in such a way. So there she clung, dozing until her grip began to slip, then waking up with a fright to re-apply it. Somehow, in one night the beautiful hills of her native land lost all of their charm.

The soft tongue on Fenner's face caused him to stir, he was wheeling and dealing, even half awake, he couldn't believe his wife had had a middle of the night change of heart with desire. He had chosen to sleep on the outside of the bed, near the door. 'In case I have to go in the night,' he had lied to Tony. Really, Fenner was worried about catching his death by sleeping next to damp wallpaper. The soft tongue tapped again, and he reached out a sleepy hand to caress his wife. He woke with a terrified start when Twinky bit his finger. Just like his wife, he had thought – until he felt a wagging tail. He sat upright in bed, his wife wore odd things in bed at night, but not a tail, even one that wagged. He groped round in the dark and felt the furry outline of the poodle. 'Bloody thing,' he hissed under his breath and felt for the end which held the collar, easing himself out of bed, and edging himself sideways along the 'gap' between his bed and the wall, dragging the dog with him. He was careful not to stub his toe on the half-open door, but fate evened the score and rewarded him by obliging him to stand on a tin-tack poking through the tattered carpet. He felt his way out on to the small landing and paused whilst his tired mind re-fashioned his memory of the landing in daylight. Opening the cupboard door where he had hung his suit, he felt down the dusty asbestos-lagged hot-water tank to the floor. 'Yes,' he whispered. 'Just enough room for a dog.' Gently pushing Twinky into a small area alongside the tank and under his suit, he closed the cupboard door quietly and, remembering to avoid the tin-tack, stubbed his naked toe on the bedroom door.

Paddy and Lynn slept sweetly and soundly, cuddled snuggly together at the bottom of their bed's valley. No thoughts of clippering round the Horn here, crashing boulder-like into the dried river bed below, or even walking a lonely poodle – all was peace in this bed. Lynn, like all the young and, supposedly, innocent could sleep anywhere and through anything, and Paddy always slept peacefully, secure in the knowledge that whatever penny-pinching scheme Fenner had up his sleeve she would counter it with a pound-pinching one of her own, backed by the full force of the Union and guaranteed to leave Fenner, the managerial arch enemy, a frustrated and grovelling loser.

CHAPTER FOUR

The drive to the Exhibition the next day was made in silence. Everybody had been glad to get up, and breakfast had thankfully been only toast and tea, and as very few people could ruin toast and tea, everybody crunched their way through different colours and textures of the stuff washed down by hot tea. Each one of them was again alone with his thoughts, and the entire staff of Fenner Fashions were 'liverish' including Twinky, who was not only doggy 'liverish' but had to bear an extra coating of dusty asbestos which gave him the distinction of being the only 'grey' poodle in captivity. Fortunately for Twinky, his doting mistress gently combed him back in patches to his natural colour, now a lightish grey. The van travelled through the busy morning streets of Southampton with an air of high tension inside. If only the innocent inhabitants of Southampton had known that a prospective 'time bomb' of pent-up emotion was being carried through their city in a furniture van, to a man they would have boarded up Bar Gate once more to repel the invaders of their peaceful and beautiful inheritance. Of course, none could know, so on went the van with its smouldering content of emotion until it reached its destination – the Exhibition of 'Buy British' for which they had all personally given so much.

The hustle and bustle of last minute adjustments in the Exhibition Hall seemed to relax the girls a little as Fenner and Tony led them to their stand. They walked in silence, admiring the beautiful wares on show and mentally arranging them on their individual sideboards and mantelpieces. They looked at the sales staff on each stand, all dressed in their best with name plates pinned to their lapels, which afforded everybody an air of informality and friendliness. The badges were not as useful as they at first seemed because it meant a customer had to address the sales people, looking at coat lapels or left boobs whilst they read their names. Still, it all added to the fun and colour but most of all it was different, because for the first time, Fenner Fashions would be 'on show' and not completely tucked away in a dingy factory back street. As the girls walked along they each realized the fact they were 'on show', and half-concealed hands checked hair and clothes, and even more concealed handbag mirrors checked make-up and eyelashes; the effect of it all was telling on the girls, and though Fenner wouldn't even know, the effect on the girls was most pleasing to them.

Fenner led them up on to 'their' stand. Now they were above people on the hall floor, and even more conscious of their appearance as they looked about them, each with a feeling that they were on at the London Palladium in front of an admiring audience of thousands – one could almost hear the preening.

'You'll be working in here,' said Fenner as they made their way through a set of curtains at the back of the stand and down a few steps. He stood in the temporary workroom holding back the curtains for the girls to enter. The girls' previous feelings fell at least ten points as they peered into the workroom area. Here it was, the same workroom bench and the same machines positioned either side, and the same workroom chairs for the girls to sit at, opposite their usual co-workers. Parole had not been granted. They had spent time 'outside' seeing things that normal people saw, trees, children, shops, etc., and now the 'warden' was leading them back to their 'cells'. That's really how the girls felt after their brief moment of imaginary glory, thinking they also might be 'on show' – but no, they were the backroom girls, others would be presented to the Queen to receive honours, they would only stand seventeen rows back in the crowd and watch their thunder being stolen. The girls filed back down the steps into the workroom in silence, and all turned as the curtains fell together with a 'clang' and the outside world was shut out from their gaze.

'We can't work in here,' said Paddy fighting back after her own happy illusion had been shattered.

'Why not?' replied Fenner, looking round the curtained workroom area.

'It's . . . er . . . too hot.' Any excuse would do for a start.

'We'll all roast with these lights and curtains,' said Kathy, mourning her own illusion.

'I'll faint,' said Olive with a tear in her eye.

'So will I,' said Jo-Jo, as she sympathetically watched Olive's mascara run.

Fenner waited for Lynn and Mabel to speak; he smiled when they didn't, not knowing they were too unhappy to do so. 'But girls,' he said, holding this bit in reserve. 'How can it be?' He outstretched a hand to the heavens.

All the girls looked up and saw the vast expanse of ceiling towering high above them, tall and most of all, airy. The curtained area of the workroom was roofless and would allow all the heat and smoke to rise and disperse in the immenseness of the hall. Defeated, the girls flopped into their chairs, with not one thought of a handbag mirror or preen among them. Fenner sensed their dilemma and called for that stalwart reviver for British people with their backs to the curtained wall – TEA. Gladly he offered to pay for it, and to show his goodwill still further, he sent Tony to get it. At length, after their tea, the girls felt much better and began to sort out 'their' workroom to 'their' satisfaction. The conversation and comradeship of the girls soon appeased their earlier disappointments. After all, they were all together in known surroundings, but a different place, and this seemed to add a happy edge to the start of their day. Fenner and Tony meanwhile were 'out front', finishing off on the stand. To the girls 'he' was in his office, Twinky was in his box, they were in their 'room', and no doubt God was in his heaven and everybody had the good feeling that Fenner Fashions was about to become INTERNATIONAL.

A tall attractive girl walked along the aisle between the stands at the exhibition. Her short 'Purdy' hair supported a small sailor hat, and her matching jacket and trousers, also in sailing fashion, completed the outfit, which fitted her elegant form. Over one shoulder hung a navy blue tote bag and in her hand she carried a small 'models' box. 'Good morning,' she said to a gaping Fenner. 'I'm Victoria Du Pree, and I'm looking for Mr Fenner.'

'Oh, I am she ... er he,' he stammered, admiring her very attractive face and smiling eyes.

'I'm from the modelling agency,' she said sweetly.

'Oh yes, of course.' Fenner offered his hand to assist her on to the platform. 'This way, Miss Du Pree,' he said with aplomb.

'Call me Vicki, please Mr Fenner,' she invited.

'Oh ... er, Harold,' he said sheepishly. 'Well, these are some of the numbers I'd like you to show.' Ignoring Tony who had placed several dummies wearing Fenner creations at various places around the stand. 'I'm sure you'll make them all very much more attractive Miss ... er ... Vicki,' said Fenner flatteringly.

'Thank you,' said Vicki. 'And where do I change?'

'Oh yes, of course.' Fenner moved to the back curtains and drew them to one side for her to see in.

'In the workroom?' said Vicki peering through.

'Oh, no. In here,' he said, descending the steps and pulling back one of the 'wall' curtains of the workroom, to reveal another curtained room complete with dress rack, long mirror, a comfortable armchair and a lighted pink dressing table and seat. 'Thank you. That'll do fine,' she said, ignoring the workroom girls, as she swept into the comfortable 'room' and looked around her.

'Well,' said Fenner leading Vicki out to the stand, 'I'll take you for morning coffee before we start.'

'Thank you,' she replied and took his arm and headed for the restaurant area.

'She's a snooty one,' said Jo-Jo.

'She gets morning coffee,' said Paddy in a posh voice. 'We get a bloody mug of tea.'

'Look at that room she's got in there,' said Kathy, pulling the curtain to one side.

'It's nicer than my bedroom at home,' said Olive sadly.

'I think I'd rather sleep there than in the hotel,' said Lynn, with good reason.

'Typical Fenner,' said Paddy. 'We do all the work and girls like her get the gravy.'

'I wouldn't mind so much but she completely ignored us,' said Mabel. 'We're as good as her any day.'

'Well some of us are,' said Paddy.

'You'd be a bit old for modelling, Mabel,' added Kathy nicely.

'I don't think I'd like to do it,' said Mabel, 'showing myself off to everybody like she does.'

'I don't know,' said Paddy, 'it might have done you a bit of good, showing yourself off.'

'Yes,' said Jo-Jo. 'You might have attracted some nice husband.'

'What good would that have done me?'

'A damn sight more than that poodle of yours could.'

'You know,' said Paddy, holding up a creation, 'I can't see her getting into this.'

'Oh, I don't know,' said Kathy. 'She's got quite a trim figure.'

'Yes, but you wait till her girdle comes off, you'll hear the bang for miles,' came the reply, amid laughter from the girls.

'Catty lot,' said Mabel, thinking about her husband that might have been if she'd have shown off a bit more.

'No,' said Lynn. 'She'd be about thirty-six bust wouldn't she?'

'Yes. And that's only one of them.'

Fenner entered the restaurant area with Vicki on his arm; she was a stunning girl and he knew it. In fact he enjoyed the turned heads of the elder male management of Bootles as he entered. Placing an order for coffee Fenner and Vicki sat at an empty table, but before the coffee arrived, all the empty seats were taken by men approaching Fenner with inane questions just to sit at his table, and be nearer to Vicki. At first, Fenner was pleased to make the acquaintance of some of Bootles' management. It would do only good in cementing their business relations. However, after a while he found himself at the back of the crowd of Vicki's admirers and felt his own importance waning fast. After all, he thought in the back row, it was me who had booked her to be here in the first place. Look at them, he thought, stupid old men. Why was it that elder men always became silly in the presence of a nice looking young girl? Everything they said had a double meaning; they laughed and chatted endlessly about nothing, always giving the impression that they were all rich and famous. Whereas he, Harold J. Fenner, owner of Fenner Fashions, by kind permission of his mother-in-law's money, had to play second fiddle to these mere employees.

Having wrested Vicki from the admiring chatter of the Bootles' men, Fenner led Vicki back to the stand. He looked at his watch; it was just before nine. He knew that as the exhibition was open to the public at nine, all his staff must be on their marks ready to go, and it would be him who would get them all cracking. This was his exhibition, it was his hour of need that would be fulfilled right here in this very hall; he had everything staked for this effort, and when that clock struck nine, it would signal the start of the 'Battle of the Bulges' all crammed into Fenner Fashions International's dresses, and all that foreign currency would be crammed into Fenner-fashioned trousers. The commander eyed his troops, he paced the waiting line eyeing them with a pound note sign in each eye. 'Now girls,' he said, 'the hour approaches.'

'Yes, dinner hour,' interrupted Paddy.

'No this is serious. Now here's the plan – we will stage a fashion show every hour on the hour lasting for about twenty minutes.' He began to fidget as Paddy made notes, but went on. 'Tony will help me out here, announcing the dresses and taking the orders from the buyers. Victoria will show the dresses dashing back to change after each one.'

'Who'll help me dress?' asked Vicki.

'Ah,' said Fenner – his first problem. 'All right. Look, Olive, you help Vicki dress.'

In the panic he'd dropped the formal Victoria and used the handy Vicki. Anything to save anything, thought Fenner. 'Now . . .' he began.

'Just a minute Mr Fenner,' interrupted Paddy.

Here it comes, he thought quickly.

'You want Olive as a dresser?'

'Yes that's right . . . now . . .'

'Then we'll have to negotiate a rate for her and us.'

'Her. All right, maybe. But US?' he queried.

'Well, we'll be doing *her* work as well as our own won't we and that's extra.'

'Well, do we have to negotiate right this minute,' said Fenner, trapped.

'Not right *this* minute . . .'

Fenner breathed easier and using the same breath he continued, 'Right . . .'

'I'll give you five minutes,' added Paddy.

Fenner breathed out as if it were his last. 'Let me get on,' he begged. 'Let's not start the day with a stop.'

'Well, OK. But I've noted it in my book.'

'Right,' continued Fenner at long last. 'Where was I?'

'Fixing a rate for Olive,' butted in Tony.

'Oh, shut up. You're always talking.'

Tony stared blankly and silently.

'Now then, you other girls will be on alterations for customers to start with, and then, if we get a few quick orders, Tony will dash back and cut them out, and then you'll make them up by the time the customer calls back for the dress – OK?'

'How long does that give us?' said Paddy, making more notes.

'Can't you read?' Fenner pointed at the board. 'It says there, *Orders ready in three hours.*'

'Then you'd better change that to four hours.

'Why?'

'We're not working our dinner hour if that comes into it.'

'Then we'll work in shifts.'

'OK,' said Paddy innocently. 'You can pay us shift money on top.'

Somewhere, a distant clock struck nine. F for Fenner hour was here. The clattering of doors being opened was like the sound of loose change in the till to Fenner. At the early hour of nine o'clock there were not many people walking round the exhibition hall, but each time a few people did walk past Fenner's stand, Fenner smiled sweetly and invitingly, but as yet no one had bothered to stop and view his creations on the dummies. Suddenly his luck changed – a large lady accompanied by a small man stopped at the stand. The woman spoke to Fenner in a foreign tongue. Fenner smiled, at a loss for words. 'Pardon?' The woman repeated her strange sounding words. Fenner smiled again and fetched one of the dummies across to show off the dress, explaining the material and showing the Fenner label, which came off in his hand. He'd ordered them to be sewn loosely so foreign buyers would not know to whom to complain. The woman shook her head. Fenner lifted up the dress to show the under-stitching, and revealed the dummy's nude legs and knickerless thighs.

'Very strong,' he intimated to the woman, stretching the stitched seam. 'Strong,' he repeated as she still didn't understand. Looking round, he spied an empty paint tin left by the decorators; he picked it up and banged it. 'Strong,' he repeated agitatedly. He banged it again then handed it to the woman; who in obvious disgust took it and threw it at his head and stormed off.

'My vife vants de toilet,' said the small husband as he followed his disappearing wife.

Fenner looked about him; he saw a few people wandering around the other stands and some even buying things.

'Why don't they come over here?' he asked Tony.

'Well there's nothing to attract them is there?'

'What do you mean, nothing to attract them?' said Fenner annoyed. 'What about all these dresses?'

'I don't mean that,' said Tony. 'I mean initially, like a bit of music for instance; you can't have a fashion show without music can you?'

'You're right. I'll go and see what I can arrange,' he said jubilantly as he hurried off.

Sheikh Ali Achmud and Basil Thornton stepped from the helicopter at the Hawker Siddeley airfield at Dunsfold, near Guildford. The sheikh's great interest in the Harrier jump jet had led Basil to arrange a flying visit in more ways than one to Hawker's airfield where the sheikh could see a Harrier in action. Basil and some other officials had fussed around the sheikh, much to his annoyance and it was only Hawker's field executive Jack Vanner, who stepped in to save the day for England and

Basil. The sheikh readily greeted Jack, whom he had met during one of his trips to Arab countries some years earlier and the two chatted warmly. Basil's warm 'collar' began to cool, and he was pleased that the sheikh had taken a revived interest in his visit, thanks to Jack. I mean, thought Basil, if he had a ride in a Harrier, or even bought one, it would be a tremendous feather in my bowler. The visit, though short, was very successful, as the sheikh had asked for further details on the aircraft to be sent to him. The 'chopper' took off from Dunsfold, everybody waving at everybody else. But Basil was only waving at Jack.

'Well, I hope something happens soon,' said Paddy.

'So do I, I'm bored,' said Kathy, filing her nails.

'I keep thinking about my lost sleep,' said Jo-Jo, whose knitting needles clicked endlessly.

'I'm thinking about our lost bonuses if something don't happen,' said Paddy.

'Mind you,' said Mabel, giving Twinky a 'drinky', 'it's nice and quiet for a change.'

'Ah, that's it,' said Paddy.

'What? Do you want a drinky as well?' said Kathy, giggling at Mabel's baby talk to Twinky.

'No stupid, quiet. We've got no music while we work.'

'But we're not working,' said Olive.

'I've got my shoes on but I'm not running,' retorted Paddy sarcastically. 'Where's Fenner? I'll see him about this.'

'He's out there winning the dress war,' said Kathy blowing a painted nail.

'In that case,' said Paddy, parting the exit curtains, 'I'll tell him the munitions girls want music while we work.'

The girls all laughed as she left.

'All right,' Fenner was saying to the Hi Fi salesman. 'You lend me the record player and some records for nothing and I'll put up a card saying music supplied by you, how's that?'

'Yes, that's fine. But you must pay for any breakages,' the salesman said clearly.

'Done. But there won't be any breakages, I'm only going to play records.' He collected the record player and went to leave. 'Where's the records?' he asked.

'They're stored inside the lid; all you need to do is plug in, put a record on and away you go.'

A free anything always pleased Fenner, and so as he approached the Fenner stand, he was smiling. 'Hello Paddy, dear,' he said seeing her on the stand. 'All working hard, I hope?'

'No, I've called a halt.'

'What's the matter now?' The smile on Fenner's face hit his shoe.

'Well, we've got no music to work to in the workroom, so we've stopped.'

'We're not back at the factory now, dear. I can't just snap my fingers and there's music.' He snapped his fingers for all Southampton to hear.

'Well that's it then,' said Paddy, producing her whistle when Tony, who had been standing near, suddenly said, 'I see you've got the record player then?'

Fenner's mind started to clear. 'What record play . . .' he began, then the pieces fitted. 'I was saving it as a surprise, wasn't I, Tony?'

'Yes, Mr Fenner,' lied Tony.

'This time you needn't have bothered to ask,' and he held up the record player with one hand and opened the lid with the other. Paddy's whistle fell limp on the string round her neck. 'Well, it's not the same,' she started. 'But it's better than nothing.'

'You can let it serve both purposes,' suggested Tony. Yes, thought Fenner, kill two birds with one free stone. Um, perhaps there's management in him yet. 'It's a good job I got it you know, Tony, and just in time,' he said as he followed Paddy to the workroom to set up the player.

The expected crowds of customers began to arrive in the Exhibition Hall – the busy cross channel ferries were arriving, bringing the early morning travellers and shoppers, and this was having an increased effect on the numbers of people coming to the exhibition; the hall was filling nicely and so were the tills.

'No, not like that, woman,' said Vicki, as Olive tried to guide her neck into the armhole of a dress. She had raced in from the 'stage' to change into the dress whilst Fenner kept the gathered audience busy with dress patter. The first fashion show was in progress and had attracted a nice crowd. The girls in the workroom were busy with alterations, and the music on the record player completed the whole, like custard on a trifle.

'Oh, Christ. Now you've torn the bloody thing.'

'Shall I get a needle and cotton?' dithered Olive.

'We haven't got time for needle and cotton – get a pin or something.' Vicki struggled the rest of the way into the tight dress, calling after Olive, 'Safety pin.'

'She doesn't half swear,' said Olive to the busy girls in the workroom.

'Well swear back,' said Paddy as her machine whirred at high speed to finish a seam.

'I don't know any swear words,' pleaded Olive innocently.

'Well, think rude things at her,' said Kathy, tossing a finished dress to the centre of the work table.

'I thought she seemed quite nice when she first arrived,' mourned Olive.

'They're all the same those birds – all greed and girdle,' said Paddy.

'She's another Mrs Fenner ain't she?' suggested Kathy.

'Oh yes,' said Jo-Jo. 'She used to be a model.'

From the dressing-room Vicki screamed out, 'Olive, where's the bloody safety pin?'

Olive shook in her tights and trotted back.

'Such a refined type,' said Lynn in a posh voice.

'Young girls didn't ought to swear like that,' said Mabel.

'Ow,' came a sceam from the dressing-room.

'What's she screaming about now?' said Jo-Jo, startled at the scream. 'She's got the pin.'

'Well, knowing Olive, she's got it all right, probably through the bum,' said Kathy.

'Yes,' laughed Paddy. 'She sent for the pin and now she's got the needle.'

The girls all laughed at this, but the laughter died as the struggling Vicki rushed from the changing-room cursing, then stood for a few moments to compose herself and then in her most innocent and sweet smile, she stepped on to the stage through the parted curtains.

'Two-faced cow,' said Paddy bluntly after the disappearing model.

'Yes,' said Kathy, thinking, and she looks a bit like Mrs Fenner as well.

'Now here is Victoria wearing a pretty little number,' began Fenner at the microphone, addressing the prospective customers gathered before the stand. 'One of Fenner Fashions most popular range.' As he said this, Victoria stepped, walked and twirled as models do, the only difference being that she was more interested in showing off 'her' and not the dress. 'Music,' screamed Fenner harshly out of the side of his mouth at Tony. 'Music,' he repeated in such a strained manner that he was almost sure that something inside him had 'gone'. What and where he didn't care; all he wanted was music for his fashion parade. Tony quickly dived his head between the back curtain and in turn screamed, 'Music.'

It had been Olive's job to put the records on between changes, but as she was in an agitated state from Vicki's understandable impatience, she had forgotten.

'Quick,' Paddy ordered Mabel who was nearest. 'Start the player, there's a record on it.' Mabel's shaking hand switched it on.

There are several things in this world that are difficult to do – one is to climb Mount Everest backwards; two, is to kick-start a Jumbo Jet single-footed; getting money out of Fenner is also in this class, but probably the most difficult thing to do is to elegantly and daintily model a very tight Fenner dress to the strains of Colonel Bogey, played by the Massed Bands of the Irish Guards. Fenner's patter was drowned by the volume and for all anybody knew, he could have been giving a talk on the sex life of a dung beetle. His horror slowly began to turn to shame which slowly turned to rage. The horns of evil which to him appeared to have grown to six feet each in length above his eyebrows, were nowhere near as ugly as the sight of Olive when Fenner had finished with her. But for the time being, all he could do was to shout up and persevere with his show. The loud opening bars of Colonel Bogey had buckled Vicki's high heels. She staggered and swayed to regain her balance in a most unlady-like way, more like the actions of a gymnast on the double bars. But then the 'Olgas' of this world wore an elasticated leotard for this cavorting, not a tight Fenner Fashions dress held perilously together not only by a safety pin in a very strategic place, but by very doubtful stitching too. She knew Fenner dresses were renowned for their unreliability. If ever a newspaper headline carried a rape story which said *The victim's dress was ripped off in seconds,* one could be sure that it was a Fenner dress. Probably the rapist had only kissed the girl lightly on the cheek, and the dress fell off in fright.

Fenner was also doing some cavorting of his own; he continued speaking to the audience through the microphone, smiling at them, and snarling towards Tony to say, 'Do something quickly or I'll rip out your black laughing heart.'

'As you can see,' continued Fenner, 'this little number is ideal for any occasion.'

'Yers, like marching down the Mall,' called a man from the crowd.

Fenner ignored him, but not before he had a quick thought, that he would like to be present when the man was devoured by a polar bear.

'The easy lines do a lot for a girl's figure,' Fenner shouted above the persisting Colonel Bogey, 'and the full back is a joy to behold.' He signalled for Vicki to do a twirl so customers could see the back. As Vicki turned, 'ping' went the safety pin and struck a passing pensioner; and see the back they could – Vicki's back, bared to the elastic of bra and knickers. She was undone, but in her own undoneness, she vowed that Fenner would be 'done' well and truly.

'Oi, guv!' called the polar bear's meal from the crowd. 'Your full back ought to be in the ladies' team according to her shorts.'

Suddenly Colonel Bogey was brought to a halt as Paddy tore the automatic record player arm across the disc, sending a loud screeching noise through the hall, shattering three wine glasses on the glassware stand at the other end of the hall. The sudden halt of the Irish Guards had left Fenner screaming at the top of his voice, '. . . and very cheap too.'

'Yes,' said a lady in the audience as she turned away from the stand in disgust. 'Very cheap.' Her departure started an exodus from the Fenner Fashions' stand, just as though some shocked school teacher had ordered her entire class on their day's outing away from this rude sideshow. Fenner watched the disappearing customers and in his heart he was sure he heard it ring up 'No Sale'.

Vicki stormed from the platform, one hand behind her back to clasp together the fast collapsing dress. Fenner's microphone hand and arm fell to his side with a clonk of metal mike on knee over the speakers. Tony had beaten a retreat with the Irish Guards. The stage was empty save for a dejected Fenner and a bent safety pin. His heart stopped for a third time as the well-known strains of Acker Bilk's 'Stranger on the "Floor" ' piped its way mournfully through the loudspeakers.

'You did it on purpose,' Vicki screamed hysterically at the girls. 'You've ruined my reputation.'

'Don't be silly,' said Paddy. 'That was ruined years ago.'

'I know your types. You're jealous, you'd like to be out there on show,' she spat with a hint of truth.

'Rubbish,' said Kathy indignantly. 'I wouldn't show my bum to a crowd.'

'And nor would I, if it hadn't been for your bad workmanship.'

'To say nothing of your oversized bum,' volunteered Jo-Jo.

'Any dress would burst with a bum that size,' said Lynn.

'Now now,' said Mabel to Lynn quietly as she held her hands over Twinky's ears. 'You shouldn't take part in this sordid argument, a young girl like you.'

'And as for that stupid cow, Olive,' raged Vicki. 'She ought to be arrested for imbecility.'

Olive started to cry and emitted a long wailing moan which alarmed several salesmen on a nearby stand, who thought it sounded like the 'bomb warning' hooter.

'Olive was doing a temporary job,' defended Paddy.

'I should think her whole brain is temporary,' said Vicki.

At this, the 'bomb warning' hooter wailed even louder as Olive flopped into her workroom chair, sobbing.

'And you're supposed to be professional,' said Kathy.

'Yes,' said Paddy sarcastically. 'She's a pro all right.'

'Oh,' said Vicki, breathing in so deeply, her bra popped. 'So now it's insults is it, you workroom waster?' She clutched and steadied her drooping boobs.

'We've seen your sort before,' said Jo-Jo still machining.

'Yes,' said Kathy checking a nail on the finger she had just painted. 'We know all about your lot.'

'Nothing more than a Fashion House Floozy,' said Paddy evilly.

Mabel 'tut-tutted' and took a firmer grip over Twinky's ears as the dog began to shake.

'And you're just a working-class factory tart,' said Vicki.

'Right, that does it,' said Paddy rising menacingly and advancing towards her. She picked up the record player and hurled it, the Irish Guards and Acker Bilk, at Vicki, standing with her back to the curtains. Hearing the noise coming from the back of the stand, Fenner parted the curtains to see if he could help. He helped all right – he stopped a flying record player from reaching the far side of the exhibition hall with his chest. Any man who stops a charge of the Irish Guards deserves to lay breathless and unconscious on the stand floor.

'Well it's not a complete write-off,' said Fenner to the Hi Fi salesman as he handed him a very bent record player. 'I mean the lid's repairable, and this Gracie Fields record's OK . . . I mean you'll get rid of that, they're good sellers you know.'

The salesman didn't speak. He couldn't. He just stood there looking at the tattered heap of 'toot' that had once been capable of throwing musical delights to all around, and now it was doubtful if it could produce a squeak from its curved record deck of spun steel. 'You've only had it about an hour,' he wailed, 'and look at it . . . a write-off.'

'Look,' said Fenner. 'Any "after tea" electrician with a screwdriver could fix it.' He tried to make his case sound plausible.

'No way,' said the salesman adamantly. 'That little lot's got to go back to the makers for repairs.' His face became set.

'All right, all right,' said Fenner anxious to get on with the 'Show'. 'I'll pay for the repairs – now where was it made?' He reached into his deep pocket for his rarely seen money.

'Taiwan,' said the salesman, taking several more ten-pound notes including Fenner's two one-pound notes.

'Taiwan! That's the other side of the world isn't it?'

'Right the other side.'

'Why couldn't you have given me an English model, made in Luton or somewhere near – Bloody Taiwan.'

'That, Mr Fenner, is the whole essence of this exhibition, to get people to buy British.'

'Then what are you doing selling that thing from Taiwan, that's not in England.'

'That, Mr Fenner, happened to be my own set.'

Fenner selected another player and checked that it was made in England – Luton if possible, or nearer – but this time he had to pay cash in advance. They'll never believe I've had to buy two record players on expenses,' he said to himself as he made his way along the aisles to his stand.

'Could I have a word with you Mr Fenner?' said a stout bald-headed, pin-stripe-suited man.

'Oh, the young Mr Bootle isn't it?'

'Yes, Mr Fenner,' said the young Mr Bootle, gravely. 'I'm afraid I've had quite a few complaints from the salesgirls on the stands either side of yours.'

'Oh, really? What's the problem?'

'Language!'

'Oh, yes. I've had the same trouble with a foreign lady who really wanted the toi . . .'

'Bad language Mr Fenner,' said Bootle, looking around him as he mentioned those two rude words.

'Oh,' half-admitted Fenner, thinking back to recent events.

'I really must ask you to keep your girls a little more in order verbally . . . I mean those curtains are only thin you know.'

'Yes.' Fenner was already backing away. 'I'll have a word with them,' he backed further away.

'Oh, there's just one other small point,' said Bootle advancing at Fenner's retreat. 'There's a long low howl that must come from a dog – it happens to be the same tone as our bomb scare warning.'

'Oh, that'll be Olive.'

'Fine,' said Bootle, now from a distance to Fenner. 'Then just give Olive a few doggie biscuits and keep it in its kennel on a lead.'

'Yes,' said Fenner out of earshot. 'That would be a good thing for Olive.'

He walked along the rows to the stand, and saw them crowded with visitors, and they all seemed to be buying. He thought about his own situation; things had gone reasonably well for Fenner Fashions at the start of the day and had only come to a crashing end when Olive got in a tangle with Vicki. Now, after all that, Vicki had left claiming her full fee, and Fenner was model-less. He would soon have to put on the next show, but how could he without a model? He stared at passing girls, his eyes working like tape measures to see if any of them would like to take on a quick job as a model. The girls returned his looks with a 'dirty old man' glare and he got more than that when he asked a girl innocently if she'd 'like to earn a few bob this afternoon'. Things are really desperate, he thought, as he rubbed his stinging face from her slap. He doubted if the agency would send anybody at such short notice especially after Vicki's report which, knowing her, she would undoubtedly file. He mustn't fail, he thought to himself. He had grabbed at this opportunity for survival and it rested on his shoulders alone to make a success of it. After all, he had a wife, mother-in-law and a bank manager to support. Dealing with Paddy would be a pleasure rather than deal with his own women folk if everything went wrong. No, come on Harold, he thought, let's pull something out of the fire. He had been in scrapes before but each one had seemed to get worse, but at least this time he would not be under the evil eyes of his wife or mother-in-law; he was away from home and at least that was a blessing in such a spot as this.

'Poor old Fenner,' said Kathy after a busy silence from the girls. 'I feel sorry for him sometimes.'

'So do I,' said Lynn, pausing as she stitched a long hem on her machine.

'Well, he does bring it on himself at times don't he?' said Paddy, not so easily sympathetic as the others. Well she couldn't be, she thought. It was no good her having too much sympathy for Fenner; after all it was her as shop steward that had to deal with him over their rates of pay and conditions, and if she got a bit soft, he would soon take advantage of the situation. On the other hand, she thought, that cow Vicki had given him a hard time and he'd taken it, but Paddy hadn't. No jumped-up model bird was going to get the better of her, and she hadn't. The girls worked on dress alterations and Tony was cutting out some more dresses in answer to the morning's orders. Busy at their work, they all had a chance to reflect on the events so far. Some kept their thoughts to themselves and worked in silence, but Kathy and Jo-Jo liked to chat as they worked. Olive, on the other hand, liked to listen to the conversation, and slip in a few comments as it went along; unfortunately for Olive, her powers of concentration were not as strong as Kathy's or Paddy's, and so there were times when one of Olive's comments stunned the conversation in its tracks. Mabel was less talkative than the others, for she thought some of the conversation was quite lewd, but she thought a lot, and in a strange way Mabel had learned a great deal about life in the raw from listening to the girls, so perhaps it was as well for Mabel, for her still tongue had made her head wiser.

'Mind you, Pad,' said Kathy. 'That Vicki's made me feel more sorry for Fenner than usual.'

'I reckon I could model as good as her,' said Lynn looking down on her own trim figure.

'Well, why don't you have a try?' asked Paddy.

'Yes, go on, Lynn,' said Jo-Jo. 'That's just what Fenner needs, a new model; here's your chance.'

'Do you really think?' said Lynn laughing at the thought.

'Sure,' said Paddy. 'You'd get model's money as well.'

'Go on, Lynn,' encouraged Kathy. 'It'll keep Fenner's money in the family so to speak.'

'She wouldn't have to do nude modelling would she?' said Mabel, caring for the young.

'Don't talk wet,' said Paddy shortly. 'Fenner flogs dresses, not skin.'

'I wonder what my mum would say,' Lynn asked shyly.

'We're not going all the way back to London to ask her; besides she'd never know,' said Kathy.

'You'd be doing it for us really, Lynn,' said Paddy.

'How d'you mean?' said Jo-Jo.

'Well, if old Fenner don't sell any dresses, we won't get any bonus.'

A silence fell on the girls. Here was a very good point Paddy had raised; now it wasn't just a case of getting Lynn to model out of sympathy for Fenner, it had become imperative to their earnings. Each of them had decided that it was the best thing for everybody. Lynn began to worry about the importance of it all, the success of Fenner Fashions International now hung on her trembling shoulders.

'Would you really Lynn,' asked a delighted Fenner, after Paddy had told him Lynn would model for him. Mind you, thought Fenner, financially she's not a professional.

'You haven't got anybody else,' prompted Tony in Fenner's ear, which twitched.

'All right, dear, you do the modelling and I'll let you have a couple of dresses, trade,' said Fenner after a while.

Paddy picked up her whistle. 'She'll get proper model's money, or I blow.'

'No,' said Fenner desperately. 'We've already had complaints about noise and language.'

'Yes,' said Tony. 'You shouldn't swear over the mike like you do, Mr Fenner, it goes all round the hall.'

'Me?' Fenner spluttered. 'Well, never mind, we've got more important things to do.' He looked at his watch. 'We've got to put on a fashion show in a minute.'

'Then it's agreed, Mr Fenner,' said Paddy. 'Lynn will model at model's money.'

'All right,' he admitted grudgingly.

'And the same conditions,' added Paddy.

'What conditions?'

'Use of dressing-room, two helpers and dinner for all of us.'

'But you're not all models!'

We're all part of a team now, eh Mr Fenner? You always said we should be.'

'A team! Blimey, you cost more to run than Manchester United.'

'Yes, but don't forget, Mr Fenner . . .' Paddy fingered her 'strike' whistle. 'You've got the ref on your side, haven't you?'

'Have I?' said Fenner helplessly. Dinner for all, he was thinking.

'Think I'll have the duck,' said Tony as he edged away.

The strings of Mantovani's Orchestra fittingly filled the air around Fenner's stand as quite a crowd gathered for the coming fashion show. Tony was out 'front' putting the finishing touches to the dresses on the dummies. The whole atmosphere was one of great expectancy, even a tingle of excitement ran through the audience – all seemed well with the world and peace reigned supreme everywhere. Everywhere that is, except in the fitting-room back stage, where complete panic, pandemonium and turmoil reigned even more supreme. Lynn stood on a stool in the middle of a gaggle of women, all pinning, poking and talking at once. Fenner was quietly going out of his mind in the back row, shouting, pointing and warding off the back-elbowed blows from the woman in front of him.

'It's a bit tight under this arm,' said Lynn.

'Hold still,' said Jo-Jo, from somewhere in the dress's folds.

'Of course it's tight under the arm,' said Kathy excitedly. 'I've got my hand down your back trying to free the zip.'

'Is that better in the front now?' Paddy asked Olive.

'Yes, there's quite a nice crowd gathering,' said Olive, peeking through the curtains.

'No, stupid. At the front of Lynn's dress.'

'This hem'll never hold,' said Mabel through a mouthful of pins.

'You're all making it look like a maternity smock,' shouted Fenner from the back.

'Well, tell 'em she's pregnant,' said Paddy, hidden beneath the dress. Mantovani played 'Some Enchanted Evening' whilst Fenner hummed the harmony to 'Onward Christian Soldiers'. Strangely, among the turmoil, it seemed to fit.

'Bloody cheap pins,' cursed Kathy, sucking a pricked finger.

'Don't get blood on the dress,' screamed Fenner.

'We're giving you our blood now Mr Fenner,' said Jo-Jo, snipping with the scissors. '... Free.'

'They sell it in America,' mocked Paddy, elbowing Fenner's pointing finger skywards.

'Come on, hurry up,' begged Fenner. 'Mantovani's nearly finished.'

'He gets a better bonus than us,' said Paddy. 'You finished your side?' she continued to Kathy.

'Yes,' said Kathy. 'All I hope is that she doesn't sneeze.'

'Come on then, step down,' said Fenner, impatiently biting his lip.

Lynn stepped from the stool helped by five pairs of hands – all still pushing, tucking and spit-sticking Lynn and her dress into place.

'It's a bit lopsided,' screamed Fenner.

'Don't worry Lynn,' advised Paddy. 'Keep leaning to the left.'

Gingerly Lynn took her first shaky steps.

'Most un-model like,' commented Fenner.

'You're still not getting her cheaper,' chipped in Paddy.

'She'll be all right,' said Mabel comfortingly.

'She will as long as it stays on,' said Jo-Jo, still pinning.

'Well, if it don't,' said Paddy to Fenner, 'tell 'em we also make bras and knickers.'

'Very funny,' said Fenner as all the girls laughed at her remark. 'We'll probably be arrested for obscenity.'

'That'll never happen in here,' said Paddy, watching Lynn walk towards the stage curtains.

'Why not?'

'Because the security blokes here couldn't spell it.'

Sheikh Ali Achmud and his entourage arrived at the exhibition hall in his specially shipped yellow Rolls Royce. The sheikh was accompanied by Basil Thornton, his personal bodyguard – a bearded giant of an Arab – and three girls from his harem. Basil had found the sheikh's purchases of military equipment during his visit a personal triumph, for in the great world of the Foreign Office, this could well mean promotion. Basil had beamed his way into the sheikh's confidence, and it had been on his own suggestion that they were visiting the exhibition. Knowing of the Arab's total fascination for gadgets of all descriptions, and here in Bootles' exhibition were all the gadgets in the world, Basil knew the sheikh would be well pleased with the visit. As the entourage moved around the stands, the sheikh made purchases which would have brought a smile to the face of the most sour-faced salesman, after a full day in dealing with the public (which had made his face sour in the first place). The sheikh never bought one of anything, one complete stand's contents, yes, but never one item. Even his Rolls was duplicated for state and private occasions. The word soon swept through the exhibition on the salesmen's telegraph grapevine. The Arabs were coming and for the retail traders: 'Happy days were here again.'

All the best goods were brought forward in profusion. To all the foreign shoppers in the exhibition hall, England was just one big happy Harrods and to all the traders, their tills were sinking slowly on the counters. Allah had not only been bountiful to the sheikh, but also to all the unfaithful on every stand in the exhibition. All except one that is. For Fenner Fashions were under heavy pressure; Mantovani had played 'A pretty girl is like a melody' four times, as the backstage girls fought like cursed disc jockeys trying to find and play a suitable musical alternative; whilst Lynn walked a model's marathon, leaning to the left and not looking a bit like a model really. Fenner, at the microphone, had gone on and on about Lynn's dress, and from that on to his other creations, and then on to the history of Fenner Fashions from the early days. The audience changed from one tired foot to another all at the same time, like a well-drilled army platoon. Fenner wasn't telling them about fashions, he was doing an act, gags, the lot. It wasn't till Tony whispered in his ear, 'They're not spending any more,' that Fenner announced the immediate entry of a new creation. As Lynn walked towards the back curtains, leaning to the left, her dress started to slip off. This unrehearsed catastrophe suddenly put new life into the waning audience, as they watched hopefully. The more Lynn walked, the more the dress slipped. As though fate was rewarding the bored audience, and as though it had all been carefully planned, just as Lynn reached the curtains, her dress fell to the floor, and a grateful audience clapped a disappearing bum enhanced by mauve knickers. Unknown to Fenner, he took the applause for himself and had the Fenner-like audacity to bow. Many hands grabbed the collapsing mauve knickers with Lynn inside, as she half-stepped and half-fell through the curtains.

'I've got cramp,' she cried as she was borne away. 'I've been all this time leaning to the left to hold the bloody dress on.'

'Never mind dear,' said Paddy, 'you did marvellous, and your end got a clap.'

'They weren't supposed to see my end,' said Lynn.

'Oh, well, that's show business,' said Kathy.

'Come on then,' said Jo-Jo. 'Let's get her changed for the next dress.'

'She looks very white,' said Mabel as they helped Lynn to the changing-room.

'I couldn't go out there again,' announced Lynn to everybody's surprise.

'You'll be all right,' said Paddy, prising off the dress.

'Yes, they've all seen you now,' said Olive holding up the next dress.

'That's just it, they've seen too much of me and I couldn't go out there again.'

'Four of the last altered,' said Tony, poking his head through the curtains and giving the sizes for the alterations. 'What's next?'

'Nothing,' said Kathy placing herself in front of Lynn's semi-nudity.

'She don't feel like doing any more,' said Paddy officially.

'She's only done one.' Tony stepped back stage. 'We can't leave Fenner sweating out there. He's said too much as it is.'

'Well, if the girl's not well,' said Mabel with concern.

'Well, somebody else'll have to do it!'

'He's right you know,' said Paddy, looking at the order sheet and thinking about the bonus. 'It's our money as well as Fenner's at stake now.'

'Come on Kathy,' said Jo-Jo holding up the next dress to be modelled.

'I couldn't get into that,' said Kathy, half-consenting. 'Besides, I wouldn't go out there on my own.'

The other girls all turned away, leaving Lynn still leaning to the left. Paddy thought deeply for one and a half seconds. 'Right,' she said with authority. 'We'll have to make up a couple of dresses out of all this material around here.'

'We couldn't stitch it that quick,' said Olive. 'To say nothing of cutting it out.'

'We won't have to.' Paddy's mind was working at the double. 'We'll just drape it around you and Kathy and say it's a new fashion. Now move.' An order was given and even Twinky jumped to attention as Paddy spoke. 'Tony! Put on a new record – something exotic. Mabel, Jo-Jo – drape this material round Kathy and Olive, and pin it. Lynn, go and get Twinky on a lead.' Paddy knew this was her finest bonus hour and was rising magnificently to the occasion. The other girls felt it also and just obeyed. 'Right, off with those dresses,' she ordered Kathy and Olive. They came off quicker than a banana peeled for a crying child. Jo-Jo and Mabel leapt at Kathy and Olive and created beautiful adornments with odd lengths of material pinned into shape; head scarves were devised, and holding a greyish poodle on a lead, the two girls stepped into the arena to the orchestral music of 'A Thousand Arabian Nights'. Their entrance brought a thunderous round of applause from the large audience. Part of that applause was for Fenner because he had stopped talking and was standing open mouthed, like a one-man petrified forest, his eyes locked on to the two amply bosomed visions of loveliness that stood tall and elegant at the back of the stand, revelling in the tumultuous reception they were receiving. This, surely, was their finest bosom hour. They liked it. The crowd liked it. And so did Sheikh Ali Achmud. Fenner's elation rose to such a pitch that he completely forgot about his audience, until Tony again whispered two little words that stimulated him into immediate action – like the prod of a bayonet from the Japanese guard's rifle. 'Money, money!'

The effect was immediate. Fenner turned smiling to his audience – opened his gaping mouth still wider to speak, but nothing came out. He was actually speechless. These were not his creations, he knew nothing about these 'dresses' – he wasn't sure if these were really his girls – what could he say about them. Whilst he was deliberating, he heard a voice through the speakers begin to give a commentary on the creations. 'Created especially for the exhibition, Fenner Fashions are proud to introduce two exclusive new gowns created in honour of all our visitors from overseas.'

Fenner turned to see who the heavenly angel was, speaking with such charm and just at the right time. Tony wasn't wearing wings nor did he have a halo about his head. What he did have was Fenner's microphone in his hand, and with the aplomb of a professional compère he related charm to the audience with his words. Fenner suddenly realized he was standing there on the stage like a spare carnation at a wedding, so as unobtrusively as he could he fidgeted and edged to one side of the stage as though led by a strange guiding hand, to the till. Tony's speech was expertly delivered, explaining the simplicity of the gowns and the uses they could be put to, and the functions they could grace. 'Kathleen is wearing our new "Night of a Thousand Eyes",' Tony went on, as Kathy, twirling, swept her attractive bulk around the stage for all to see, bringing more applause from the delighted audience who were now spell-bound at the new creations. 'Whilst Olivia,' continued Tony sexily, 'graces our show with our new "Secrets of the Sands" created for romance.'

Olive, her big moment at hand, did her twirl with grace. Unfortunately, Twinky, whom she was holding on a lead, did not twirl so gracefully and wound himself in the folds of Olive's trailing gown. The dog disappeared for a while as Olive tripped her well-proportioned self around the stage, showing her gown. At the end of Olive's pirouette, Twinky's tiny head poked through the flowing tresses at Olive's feet and looked about him at the gazing eyes of the audience. Well, what could a dog do? For the audience, he gave a yap, that brought ecstatic applause from the charmed admirers. However, for Olive, the other end of Twinky concealed under her dress, he gave a wee that brought horror and a wet leg to a brave-faced Olive. The whole short but effective fashion show had the desired effect on the onlookers, who pressed forward to Fenner's aching till finger which they kept busy with their orders for the new creations. Gone were his thoughts of wives and mothers-in-law and bank managers, bonuses and rates; Fenner, an artist in money, had set an exorbitant price on the creations in a trice. Fortunately, because of the wonderful show to which the buyers had been treated, money was no object. From the back of his mind Fenner saw he would make much profit. From the back of the stand, another knew that much profit was to be had, for Paddy watched with eagerness through the slightly parted curtains at their success. She also was an artist, in rates and bonuses and she had set a price for it all in half a trice.

Kathy and Olive returned backstage in triumph; there was no need to continue showing any other dresses – the front of the stand was being inundated with orders; it didn't matter anyhow – success from everybody's efforts had seen to that, they'd cracked it. The girls jabbered joyfully, as they helped Kathy and Olive unwind from their creations.

'Bespoke without a stitch,' said Kathy as she revolved to unwrap her shapely form from the fashionable 'bandages'. Olive also was unwound not only from the material, but from Twinky's lead, that had wrapped around her feet, causing her to walk like a dainty eleven-stone geisha girl. Twinky was patted all round and feted.

'Oh!' said Jo-Jo to a delighted Mabel, who was crooning, 'There, there, my baby,' into the dog's ear. 'Give him a toffee, he's done well.'

'Give him a po, he's done a wee,' complained Olive, stripping off a soggy pair of tights.

'That's for good luck,' chirped Paddy, gloating over their happy success.

'Christ,' said Olive. 'I'm only glad it wasn't a Great Dane.' They chatted on gaily about the events, how Fenner had dried up on the microphone.

'Lost for words,' said Lynn, the ex-model.

'He stood there as though his wife was giving him one of her lectures,' said Kathy, climbing back into her own clothes.

'And how about that Tony?' said Jo-Jo spraying a deodorant on Olive's legs. 'He'll be at the Palladium next as a compère.'

'Watch out, Bruce,' said Paddy. 'You've got a rival.'

'That dog won't pee every performance will it?' said Olive to Mabel.

'Oh, no,' said Mabel, still whispering sweet 'mummy' phrases into the dog's ear. 'It was the excitement that made him do it.'

'Good job for Twinky that Olive didn't get excited,' said Lynn coming out of her shell at the happy banter.

The girls screamed with laughter and then even more at the look on Olive's face. 'Blimey,' she said. 'The things I do for Fenner.'

'Yes, but think of all the lovely bonus we'll get,' said Paddy, helping Olive back into her own clothes.

'What's the rate for a dog peeing up yer leg?' giggled Jo-Jo to Paddy.

'I don't know,' tittered Paddy. 'I'll ask Littlewoods, they know all about pools.'

Out on the stand, Fenner and Tony were having a field day. They had taken orders galore for the new creations. Buxom German ladies found the wrap-around gowns ideal for camouflaging their ample frames. Women of all sizes could enhance or reduce their endowments to suit their wishes with the easy-fitting materials. Fat ladies could become elegant; thin ladies could become cuddlesome; short and fat ladies could all share in the glory of looking how they wanted to look, and not how they did in reality. Fenner Fashions had blazed a trail of freedom for ladies of awkward sizes. Fenner had liberated half of Europe and never fired a shot. It was a complete vindication of his plan to wrest Fenner Fashions out of the money mire; he could stand tall in his socks, measure up to his wife and mother-in-law and bank manager. They would cower in awe before him as he rode home triumphantly – lying on a bed of money – on a litter carried by the girls – counting. He would become a tycoon, a force to be reckoned with. 'Don't trifle with Fenner,' they would say, 'Or he'll break you into pieces – with his money bag.'

As he dreamed his way through the Casino at Juan les Pins, squandering one franc pieces with gay abandon to the gasp of the idolizing crowd, Fenner hardly heard Basil Thornton say to him, 'Mr Fenner, may I introduce Sheikh Ali Achmud?'

Fenner didn't hear most of the introduction from Basil, but

what he did hear in his jumbled mind was 'Rich Arab'. He took the sheikh's hand and, not knowing whether to bow or curtsy, he did a sort of bowing curtsy in homage to the man, who ignored Fenner's peculiar gyration and merely shook hands in the time-honoured fashion observed among men of generations.

'How do you do your Sheikh . . .' Fenner bit off his tongue. How does one address a sheikh? he thought hurriedly. Your Sheikhness? Your Arabness? Your Sheep Dip? He needn't have bothered, it was too late; the moment had passed. But what about language, the sheikh couldn't speak English perhaps. What did I use to say to those Arabs in the desert during the war, he thought. Ah yes, that was it, make him feel at home. 'Torra biddy, Torra Char, Banbay Biddy, Bhote Hotcha,' he said in reasonable Hindustani.

'I'm very pleased to make your esteemed acquaintance,' said the sheikh in perfect Oxford English.

Fenner's balloon of thoughts deflated with a long low raspberry of embarrassment. 'Oh,' he said sheepishly. 'Thank you very much.'

'Yes,' added the sheikh. 'I have been most impressed with your new collection; very exciting if I may say so.'

Please do, thought Fenner, I'll just put it on the bill. 'Thank you,' he said, thinking better of it. 'Mr Thornton kindly arranged for me to visit here today,' continued the sheikh. 'And I'm very pleased your foreign office allotted such an able man to me.' Basil heard the pleasant breeze of promotion blowing more strongly through his career.

'Oh, we try to please,' said Fenner on behalf of the Foreign Office.

'And you have, Mr Fenner, for I should like to purchase your new creations.'

'Purchase' was always a pleasant word to Fenner especially from a wealthy Arab, he thought, looking at his three harem attendants. 'Three new dresses would be a nice sale, he thought, especially if he made it six – one on and one in the wash.

'I should like to dress my harem in such fine clothes,' said the sheikh.

He's going to go for six, thought Fenner gleefully. 'Er, how many would that be?' he asked gingerly.

'Well . . . shall we say six?' He's said it, thought Fenner. One on and one in the wash. 'Six?' he repeated to Tony who was poised with his order pen at the ready.

'Dozen,' said the Arab, confirming Tony's large 6 on the order pad. The bells that chimed in Fenner's head were made of solid banknotes, the heavenly choir sang 'All Hail to the Rich Fenner' in three point harmony to the accompaniment of a large piped, four-keyboard till, whose music filled the strong-room in Fenner's High Street bank.

After Fenner had landed from his tour of heaven, he asked the sheikh about sizes, etc. This would be bespoke; bespoke, he assured the sheikh, Fenner Fashions *International* are entirely at his service.

'Yes, of course,' said the sheikh. 'Come to the yacht tomorrow with the girls and their dresses and we'll sort it out there. Mr Thornton, will you give the directions? Until the morrow then Mr Fenner?'

He gave a little bow and moved on to see the rest of the exhibition, followed by his bodyguard and the three harem girls. Basil quickly gave directions and details to Tony, because Fenner was floating three metres above the stage in his own personal plane of ecstasy, then raced off to catch up with the departing sheikh.

'. . . and that's the plan, dears,' said Fenner after he had explained all the events concerning the Arab to the listening girls. 'So Paddy will come with me to do the measuring for the gowns on the Arab's yacht, along with Kathy and Olive who will model them again.

'You're not having Twinky on a yacht,' said a protective Mabel, fearing for the dog's life. 'He'd be sea sick.'

'Ugh!' said Olive.' It was bad enough him weeing over me.'

'No, we don't want any dogs on the yacht,' said Fenner. 'That's all we'd need, him peeing up the main sail, we'd be washing it for weeks.'

'And probably lose the order,' said Jo-Jo sympathetically.

'Yes. Any rate,' continued Fenner, 'Tony, Jo-Jo, Lynn and Mabel will stay here and get on with the alterations and new orders whilst we are away. OK?'

'Who'll model the dresses with you lot away?' said Tony, making a good point.

'A good point. But we shouldn't be long on the yacht, so we'll dash there and back between shows.'

It all sank in for a few minutes, and then mixed thoughts appeared on all their faces. At long last Paddy broke the silence with, 'And how much is all this dashing to and fro worth to us?'

Fenner was expecting this. 'You'll all be well taken care of.'

'Yes,' said Kathy cautiously, 'like we are in the hotel.'

Boom, went this bomb in Fenner's ears.

'Now then,' said Paddy, producing her notebook. 'We'll take care of ourselves thank you, Mr Fenner, so let's take the points slowly.'

Here it comes, thought Fenner. Here comes the plan that will give me cause to take an overdose of nerve pills, and if she blows that whistle I will just die here and now. Then he had visions of this callous lot stepping over his rotting body, being too bonus greedy to give him a decent burial, so he didn't think about dying any more, but said, 'Go on,' inviting Paddy to do so as he crossed his arms to listen.

'Well, we shall want transport to the yacht and back and travelling time.'

The other girls sat, listening and each nodded a silent, 'Yes, that seems fair.

'But you're already getting travelling time to and from the hotel.'

'Ah,' corrected Paddy. 'But this'll be outside work, so we want outside rates as well.'

'That means that you want outside, outside rates.'

'That's right,' said Kathy, supporting Paddy.

'Outside the hotel rates and now outside the exhibition rates; I shall be outside the cinema selling matches to pay for all this.'

'Now we come to modelling rates,' said Paddy reading further.

'We already agreed that when Lynn did it,' pointed out Fenner.

'Yes. But this is outside modelling now so they get extra . . . any worker required to do another worker's work when and if the first worker is not available for that work, shall get that worker's . . .'

'Yes, all right.' Over the years, Fenner had Paddy's union rule book emblazoned on his memory for all time.

'It's all work, ain't it?' said Jo-Jo to Paddy, punning the union rule.

'Yes. And it's got to be paid for . . . now. For those of us who are left here, they will be doing our share of the work, so they'll be on double time till we get back.'

'Double time! I have enough trouble getting you to work single time,' Fenner said, looking at them all in turn.

'Ah, but we've got to have incentive,' said Jo-Jo. 'We're not cheap foreign labour you know.'

'If only I could fill this place with Chinese, they make clothes to measure in an hour in Hong Kong.'

'Yes,' said Kathy, 'maybe so. But look at what you'd have to pay them in travelling time.'

'Well, you're getting nearly as much without all that travelling. So I want some efficiency and production out of you lot to pay for it all.'

'Rely on us, Mr Fenner,' said Lynn.

'I've got to,' said Fenner regretfully. 'I don't know any Chinese.'

'I wouldn't work with Chinese,' said Mabel, cuddling Twinky. 'They eat dogs.'

'They don't eat dogs,' said Kathy, putting Mabel's mind at rest. 'It's cats they eat.'

Everybody felt suddenly sick.

'Well, enough talking,' said Fenner, rising. 'If we don't get any work done, we won't be able to afford to eat.'

'We will when we get our royalties though,' said Paddy casually.

'What royalties?'

'The royalties on the dresses we've created.'

'All designers get it,' added Olive.

'Well I'm not paying out royalties.' Fenner sounded adamant.

'You'll have to,' said Paddy equally defiantly.

'Why will I?'

'Because we won't tell you how we made the dresses, that's why.'

'You wouldn't do that?' said Fenner with a look of appeal to all the girls ... 'You would!' He gave up and began to walk away. 'Come on Tony, get on the mike, it's nearly time for the next show.'

'You haven't fixed my rate yet,' said Tony not moving.

'What rate's that?' Fenner stopped in his tracks.

'Compère's rate.'

'Compère's rate? You're not a compère, you're my cutter.'

'Yes. Your *only* one, and that's why I know you'll pay me extra for compèring.'

Fenner gasped. 'I suppose you'll want a recording contract as well?'

'It's possible. I could be discovered you know.'

'You'll be discovered all right . . . missing. Now let's all get cracking, it's costing me a fortune standing here, in more ways than one.'

'Have I got to take my clothes off in front of that Arab?' said Olive to anybody that was listening.

'No,' said Fenner firmly and with an eye to business, 'don't do that, he won't look at the dresses.'

'Only I don't think my Arthur would like that,' continued Olive.

Fenner shook his head and thought this was a good time to escape, so he did, as some of the girls took their places round the workbench, whilst the others prepared for the next fashion show.

'We've done all right out of this haven't we, Pad?' said Kathy, preparing to strip.

'Yes,' she said, spotting Tony watching Kathy. 'And he's doing all right out of it as well. Hop it, Tony. Your public awaits you.' She smiled and levelled a kick at Tony's backside as he slipped out through the curtains. 'Right now, girls.' She raised her voice so everyone could hear in the workroom too. 'This little jaunt by the seaside is going to be worth a nice few bob for us, no point in going home penniless is there?'

'I'll be able to buy that washing-up machine I've been after,' said Jo-Jo dreamily from the workroom.

'Oh, what are you going to do with your old one?' asked Olive.

'Not so much of the "old",' said Jo-Jo, 'I'm the old washing-up machine in our house.'

'I don't think my Arthur's washed up once since we've been married,' said Olive mournfully.

'You ought to insist on it,' said Mabel, fitting on a new bobbin of cotton to her machine.

'I did once,' admitted Olive.

'What happened?' called Paddy so they all could hear.

'He left it all outside the back door and said a prayer for rain,' said Olive, in all seriousness.

'I'd have stopped his Nookie,' said Kathy struggling out of a skirt.

'Really! said Mabel. 'What a suggestion, and in front of Lynn as well.'

'I couldn't do that,' said Olive thoughtfully.

'Why not?' asked Lynn curiously.

'Well,' said Olive with a sigh. 'I can't stop what he hasn't started.'

'Can't we change the subject?' pleaded Mabel. 'All this talk of sex.'

''Ere,' said Kathy with a wink. 'How far's the North Sea?'

After a very long day at the exhibition, the girls packed up for the night and Tony drove them home to the hotel. Being so tired, the journey was made almost in silence, each one occupied by their own thoughts. They sat in the back of the van and dozed as they were bumped and swayed in its empty cargo space as it ground along the uneven roads. It had been an eventful day and this had glossed over their fatigue, for they hadn't noticed how tired they were until the closing hours of the exhibition's long day. As a venture, it had been successful considering the setbacks which, in their own way, they had overcome; for though they didn't always realize it, they were a team. It might have been a bit of push and shove with Fenner, as it always was, but management and workers had each got the measure of the other over the years, and the balance produced results. They all knew each other pretty well from working such a long time together, and this tempered their differences. For their circumstances always had an effect on their reactions, and since each of them also knew the others' circumstances, an even greater understanding had developed between them. It is difficult to bear a grudge against someone if you know the possible reasons for the grudge in the first place, and this was very often what happened between all parties of Fenner Fashions. So swords were often drawn, but blood wasn't. If one looked at the group of snoozing girls in the back of the lorry, one would smile with affection at each of their little idiosyncrasies, as the gaze shifted from one to the other. Remembering some particular little incident that had happened to any of them, or a story they may have related whilst sitting round their work table. The work table was the symbol of understanding between them. The pow-wow at which the pipe of peace and war often smouldered. It could have been any board table, any table at which great world events were discussed to the humble kitchen table, across which triumphs and failures, gains and losses, happiness or sadnesses were discussed, but usually most of all shared. All this, though unknown to some of the girls, was their cord of comradeship that bound them together in sisterhood, for when the working day was ended they each went their own way, alone, facing their individual battles. Fortunately, the workroom table gave them a shot in the arm that lasted them overnight, so their personal loneliness and problems to some degree diluted until the morning, when the batteries of their lives were re-charged in each other's company. So slept the girls this night: the discomfort of their stay in Southampton and the fatigue of their long day had been watered down with their companionship; the problems halved with their laughter; and the blunders overcome by their spirit. Even the dumb Twinky slept soundly in this knowledge.

CHAPTER FIVE

By the morning, the girls felt greatly refreshed after their night's sleep. They had gone to their rooms earlier than normal and literally attacked their uncomfortable beds with all sorts of ingenious ideas to improve them. Suitcases were positioned under the sagging middles, supporting them to some sort of sleepable level. Olive and Mabel's board bed had been padded by a motley collection of blankets, sheets, coats, curtains and materials from Fenner Fashions. All donated by the other girls and Fenner, so, though he didn't know it, some of his best dress material now supported 'two girls in a bed', to say nothing of the dog! Even Tony and Fenner had been inventive in making their bed more tolerable. They had stripped off the asbestos lagging pads from the hot water tanks in the wardrobe/cupboard outside their bedroom, placed them over the sagging springs in the centre of their bed, and covered the whole with the mattress. The success of 'operation bed repair' showed in the girls' happy manner as they drove to the exhibition that morning. Breakfast had improved a great deal since Paddy had a quiet word in the ear-ringed ear of the landlady, threatening to go to the TUC head office and expose her bawdy tatty house to the seaman's union, and black the Lighthouse Hotel for ever – and, if necessary, longer! Paddy knew her union stuff and her compelling manner had frightened the very false eyebrows off the 'made-up' landlady, who consequently had worn a clean pinny at breakfast that morning.

The furniture van's bumps and sways seemed to be in tempo with the girls' songs which they sang with great gusto as they travelled along, especially the rude bits. To the onlookers and citizens of Southampton who watched the furniture van sway along its way, it appeared that the 'radio' inside was on full volume, playing what seemed to be a drunken 'Nun's Chorus' singing all the rugby, army, navy and air force songs (not necessarily in that order). It gave the impression that some monster ice-cream van had been constructed and ten thousand chimes had been orchestrated for voices, capable of calling the 'faithful' kids to frozen refreshment from at least fifteen miles in any direction.

'Bless 'em all,' from the girls, brought a tear of nostalgia to the eye of a passing police sergeant who, having turned his head to the 'east' in answer to the 'call' remembered by a million servicemen, having mounted the pavement on his bike, ran into a lady with a pram.

'I was a young man again,' he pleaded with the mother as he extricated himself and his bike. 'It reminded me of my war days,' he went on, straightening his handlebars.

'Well for you they've started again,' said the angry mother as she clumped him with a carrier bag from a fashionable boutique bearing the slogan, 'Peace Brother' . . .

Having dropped Jo-Jo, Lynn, Mabel and Twinky at the exhibition stand, Fenner collected the materials and equipment needed for the visit to the Arab's yacht. Then the van made its way out of Southampton to the river moorings where *Checkmate* lay at the 'Ditty Box' in Hamble river. Tony drove the van with skill as it motored out of the city and into the countryside surrounding Southampton. The roads grew narrower as the large van turned into Hamble Lane which led to the river. As they passed a pub on the outskirts of Hamble village, the girls gave a cheer through the half-open shutter at the back of the van. The pub was called The Harrier.

This wouldn't have meant much to the girls who gave every pub a cheer out of principle, but Basil Thornton would have cheered even louder at the name 'Harrier' for that was the name of the Hawker Siddeley vertical take-off world-beater plane that the sheikh might well buy. Basil would also cheer his own career which he was confident would now improve with the sheikh's spending. The entrance to Hamble village proper and the river front was extremely narrow and Tony needed all his skill to manoeuvre the van down the lane. Normally the reserve of Rolls and Bentleys, the furniture van raised several eyebrows as it passed. The Bugle, a lovely riverside pub, outside which sat several early morning coffee types, dressed in expensive sailing clothes. The girls didn't care, they weren't proud. They gave The Bugle a cheer which raised the eyebrows even further and, unknown to them, an elderly old salt spluttered into his rum and coffee at the sight of the van, as he watched in astonishment from the Royal Yacht Club opposite. Tony parked the van and they unloaded their materials and made their way along the floating walkway which led to the 'Ditty Box' mooring of *Checkmate.* All around them were moored some of the most beautiful craft they had ever seen: huge sailing yachts with tall masts, whose stainless steel rigging wires chattered in the light breeze against the steel fingers which pointed skywards; giant diesel cruisers wallowed and lapped in the water against strained mooring ropes which secured the fantastically expensive 'toys' of those who liked and could afford to be 'messing about in boats' – clean boats of course. It seemed to the girls that the entire maritime wealth of England was moored here, and their chatter reflected their desires as they walked.

'Ooooh, I'd like that one,' said Kathy, pointing to a magnificent 'Gin Palace' craft which was receiving attention to her fenders from a young bronzed Adonis in shorts and sailing hat.

'What? That boat?' inquired Olive.

'No, daft . . . that fella on it.'

'I'd rather have that one,' said Paddy as everybody's gaze was directed to a sailing yacht nearby, whose sails were airing in the breeze. 'I could imagine myself pulling on the sheets in that!'

Olive strained her spectacles to which man Paddy wanted to pull sheets with in a love bed.

Fenner had been quiet all this while, his mind had far deeper thoughts than the girls' dreams. He also looked at the expensive craft, but it was he who tended her needs, in his mohair shorts and gaberdine captain's hat trimmed with enough gold braid to warrant a salute from Prince Philip or similar. This exhibition had been his destiny and he was fulfilling it to the full. He was being shown by the Fates what he could expect in reward for his sales success, and he gazed at the beautiful craft at anchor. It was as clear as the gold in his tooth, he could see his boat there, the *Ocean Fenner*, and in small letters underneath its name plate, *R.Y.C., Royal Yacht Club*. 'I'm delighted to have you aboard, your majesty,' he said, rising from being dubbed Sir Harold Fenner of East London. 'May I offer you a caviar sandwich?' Yes, he thought, just a humble gown merchant that supplied the world with dresses.

A tiny dinghy floated at the stern of Fenner's 'fancy' and Tony dreamed realistically about owning one like that. He could sail it on week-ends and be at peace with the world. Along quiet rivers he would drift in the warm sun and snooze as the breeze dropped to a breath. Olive's choice was a large houseboat lying on the mud; she could see herself in her apron with a large anchor embroidered on it, hoovering and dusting, whilst not far away simmered the potatoes and greens on the warm friendly stove and not much further away was Arthur having a pint and a sausage sandwich in the Royal Yacht Club, his 'local'. Yes, it would be very nice, thought Olive. Not being a very good sailor, that houseboat would be steady in that mud. She felt it would just suit Arthur and her a treat, just the sixty pounds a week mooring fees and their food and keep, and Arthur's membership to the Royal Yacht Club, and his beer another fifty-eight pounds a week – and nothing else to worry about.

Checkmate loomed ahead, so Fenner halted his party to issue his orders. 'Now look girls, we'll get all this lot on board, and then you, Tony, can get back to the exhibition and take care of things. We'll look after this end.' He was poised on the springboard of his future. 'Paddy will dress Kathy and Olive if necessary, in case the sheikh wants to see my fashions again.'

'Our fashions,' corrected Paddy.

'Our fashions,' continued Fenner. 'And then we'll measure up all his harem girls.'

'*We'll* measure the girls,' said Paddy in correction again.

'Yes,' added Kathy. 'If you mess about with the sheikh's birds, that big bodyguard will cut off your vitals.'

'All right, all right,' said Fenner pondering this point. 'Well I'll chat up the sheikh and tell him all about our good quality clothes.'

'*Good* quality,' said Paddy. 'That big bodyguard will be busy.'

'Is he what they call a eunuch?' asked Olive, remembering a film she once saw.

'I bet my Arthur'd like that job – all those girls.'

'No,' said Kathy giggling, 'your Arthur's not cut out for that job.'

'Oh,' said Olive casually.

Tony helped load the materials and equipment on to *Checkmate,* then took one look at the big bodyguard overseeing them, and fled to the safety of the van which he drove like a demon, putting as many miles between him and the sheikh's personal giant as quickly as he could. Fenner and the girls looked nervously at the exquisite luxury of the sheikh's yacht and felt they should have wiped their feet more thoroughly than they had as they stepped aboard. The sheikh stepped from the main saloon of the yacht to greet the party. 'Thank you, Abdul,' he said to the giant bodyguard, dismissing him. Fenner and the girls watched as his 'seven league' sandals carried him away and out of sight in what seemed like one step.

'Greetings,' said the sheikh, bowing in eastern tradition.

'Greetings likewise,' chorused the girls and Fenner, also bowing in the East End tradition.

'Perhaps you'd care for some refreshment before we begin?' suggested the sheikh, inviting them to enter the main saloon. Fenner and the girls ogled at the splendorous decor. Draped with silk and gold furnishings which hung in profusion, with a low-legged table and cushions as the centre piece, the whole atmosphere was very eastern and very opulent. The bright sun shone through the large porthole windows, and made the richness of the room twinkle in its rays. They seated themselves on the cushions around the table and copied the sheikh as he sat cross-legged at its head. Crossing their legs in tight skirts proved a very difficult and intricate operation for the girls and the sheikh was treated to several flashes of knicker as they did so. Though he clapped his hands for service, it gave the girls the impression that the applause was for their show of panties. Shuffling on their bottoms, the girls sank into the cushions' padded depths to retain a lady-like posture, which they achieved after several steadying hands from those sitting nearest to them. In answer to the sheikh's applause, a beautiful young Arab girl appeared carrying a tray of cups and saucers made of gold and several tall, eastern pots and jugs which she placed on the table before them. Fenner's eyes were on the newly-arrived damsel, who was dressed in a shimmering see-through silken creation of typical eastern style.

'Tea?' invited the sheikh, noting Fenner's gaze at the girl.

'Yeah,' said Fenner sexily.

'This is Jasmin, my favourite,' announced the sheikh to everybody.

Fenner looked away quickly, after giving the girl a sickly smile. He could almost hear the bodyguard whipping out his scimitar, raising it above his head to render Fenner permanently impotent.

'How d'you do love?' said Paddy admiring the silken tresses of Jasmin.

'Charmed,' said Kathy, which brought looks from everybody.

Olive reached out to shake hands and knocked a jug over on the tray which brought even more looks from everyone, while Fenner hissed through his teeth.

'No matter,' said the sheikh, 'it's only water.'

Jasmin set the cups and saucers and began to pour the tea from the ornate teapot.

'Have you a large factory, Mr Fenner?' asked the sheikh.

'Oh yes, I've only brought a small part for the exhibition.'

'And do you have many girls in your employ?'

'Oh yes,' began Fenner. 'Fifty . . . six,' said Fenner and Olive together.

Olive sunk the embarrassment in her teacup as Fenner killed her with a stare.

'And how long have you been modelling Miss . . . er?' faltered the sheikh.

'Kathy,' she said smiling.

'Kathy,' he repeated.

'Oh, I've only started . . .' she began until she was nudged by Paddy. 'Five years,' she corrected herself.

'And you . . . er?' said the sheikh, inviting Olive to speak her name.

'Same,' said Olive.

'Same? That's an unusual name.'

'No,' interceded Paddy. 'She's been modelling the same time as Kathy – her name's Olive.'

'Olive,' repeated the sheikh, 'the sun-kissed fruit of ancient Egypt.'

'Oowha,' said Olive, full of eastern promise, 'is that what my name means? – my Arthur was there during the war.'

Fenner cringed at the thought of Olive stirring old wounds between nations.

'And how about you?' the sheikh asked Paddy, steering the conversation away from war and back to names.

'Me? I wasn't in Egypt,' said Paddy firmly, as Fenner sank deeper into the cushions in shame. 'No, dear lady,' said the sheikh. 'How are you called?'

'It's all according whose calling. If it's Mr Fenner it's "oi" and if it's the girls, it's Pad.'

'Oi, Pad?' queried the sheikh, baffled.

'Yes, that's right.'

'He speaks good English for a foreigner, don't he?' said Olive.

The mouthful of hot tea that Fenner had just taken was inhaled into his lungs at Olive's remark. The searing pain in his chest exploded in a cough that caused the curtains to shiver at the windows. Paddy thumped his back, nearly dislocating his shoulderblades in an effort to restart his lungs, which felt as though they'd received a blow-back from an inflatable dinghy which he had been blowing up with his mouth. Slowly he recovered from his attack and lay gasping on the cushions. Jasmin leaned over him with a cup of water the sheikh had ordered for him. Through his half-opened eyes, Fenner saw the angel bending over him and tried to smile. What an ironic thing fate was, he thought. Just as he was about to earn a fortune, he had died in a fit of coughing caused by those factory girls. He closed his eyes again for he could not bear to swear in front of an angel whilst looking at her straight in the face. He smelt the heavenly perfume and thought he'd smelled it before somewhere on earth.

'Here,' said Paddy, taking the cup of water from Jasmin, 'let me do it.' She gently sloshed it in Fenner's face, and he came swiftly back to life when he saw that the angel's sweet face had suddenly turned to evil!

Accompanied by the bodyguard for support and Paddy and Jasmin for guidance, Fenner was taken on deck for a breath of fresh air. Meanwhile the sheikh invited Kathy and Olive to move closer to him on the cushions, 'To get to know you better,' he'd said. The heat in the room seemed to be increasing as the sheikh nestled closer to the two girls.

'It's a lovely boat you've got here, sheikh,' said Kathy, pushing his arm from her waist.

'Yes,' said Olive, doing the same. 'How many miles does it do to the gallon?'

'Your eyes remind me of the oasis,' returned the sheikh, nuzzling Olive's neck with his nose.

'Oh, does it?' She was a bit disappointed that he should compare her eyes with the Oasis Café near the factory.

'And your hair,' he murmured to Kathy, stroking it, 'is like the soft breeze of evening.'

'Oh dear,' said Kathy, who felt she could use a cool breeze right now.

The sheikh's advances had rather taken the two girls by surprise and they had both reacted differently: Olive had quite enjoyed it; but Kathy thought of her boyfriend who worked on an oil rig and if she upset the sheikh, he might get the sack, as the Arab probably owned it.

'Come with me to Arabia?' the sheikh whispered in Olive's ear.

'Ooh, I couldn't go all that way,' said Olive. 'I mean who'd get Arthur's tea?' She giggled as the sheikh's breath tickled her ear.

The sheikh was alternating his affections between the two girls, taking each into his romantic confidence in turn, as he whispered eastern praises into their western ears. At first they were taken aback by his forthrightness, but now they were getting the measure of him and though they had slightly differing opinions, it was a new and harmless experience. They were enjoying it, and they began to consider what the other girls would do in their shoes.

'I will dress you in finery,' he tempted Kathy.

'*Un*dress me, more likely,' she giggled.

The sheikh persevered, unperturbed, swooning over their beauty, and ignoring or not hearing their asides.

'It can do you nought but good,' he breathed.

'It would do Mabel good, more likely,' said Olive.

'You would fit into my life perfectly,' he went on.

'Jo-Jo would,' said Kathy.

'How do you mean?' asked Olive across the sheikh's chest.

'Well,' came the reply from under the sheikh's caressing arm, 'she's lived over that way more hasn't she?'

'Oh, is Africa over that way then?'

'Yes, sort of.' Kathy bent backwards away from the sheikh's advancing lips.

'You could bath in goats' milk,' murmured the sheikh to Olive as he blew tenderly up her nose.

'Oh, Arthur likes goats' milk,' mooned Olive, scratching her tickly nose.

'He wouldn't after you'd bathed in it,' said Kathy, prising the sheikh's hand from her knee.

Their conversation could have been heard round their work table instead of in the floating love-nest, but they continued doing gentle battle with the sheikh, at the same time talking as though he was no more than a difficult bodice or pleat they were sewing.

'I won't rush you now,' said the perspiring sheikh finally. 'We have our lives in front of us.'

'Yes,' said Kathy, 'where you've got your hands.' She pushed them away for the thousandth time.

'Look out!' said Olive. 'Here comes Fenner.' She sounded just like any of them would do if they happened to spy Fenner entering the workroom.

'That little spin round the deck did him good,' said Paddy, entering the cabin. 'It's revived him.'

'Good,' said Kathy as the three 'lovers' resumed their normal positions. 'You better take Olive and me now.' She giggled. 'Or the sheikh.'

'Why? Is he feeling faint?' said Paddy.

'No,' said Olive, as the sheikh asked how Fenner felt. 'He's just feeling.' She made a sign of groping with her hands.

'Oh, is he?' said Paddy, catching on quickly.

'Yes, I'm all right now,' said Fenner in reply to the sheikh. 'Shouldn't we get on with our work?'

'Yes, please,' said Olive, as she and Kathy sprang to their feet.

Fenner looked in amazement. He'd never seen such a quick reaction to work before in his whole life at Fenner Fashions. 'Good,' he said as the flush of money returned to his cheeks.

'The girls' quarters are through there, Oi Pad,' the sheikh said to Paddy, using her mistaken name. Paddy looked where he was pointing, ignoring the opportunity to correct her name.

'Good, then we'll get on,' said Fenner, opening the door which led from the saloon to the next cabin.

Abdul looked down on Fenner from a great height, gazing at the hair on Fenner's head, whilst Fenner gazed at the hair on Abdul's chest.

'I'm afraid that's women only,' said the sheikh.

'Oh, don't worry,' said Fenner in a jocular but assuring way. 'I have to work with women all day.' He tried to get through but walked into the wall of Abdul instead.

'It's our custom,' said the sheikh. 'Only women and me.' His eye glinted.

'Yes, you stay out of it,' said Paddy. 'We get on much better without you.' And with that, the three girls entered the harem.

'I think we'll take Abdul back with us to the factory when we go,' Paddy said, turning before she finally disappeared with the others into the 'sanctum sanctorum'.

Fenner was a bit agitated, he wasn't worried about seeing a few nude birds around, all his years in the rag trade had accustomed him to that, though he wouldn't have minded a quick peep at Jasmin starkers, he thought to himself. No, what worried him more was the amount of material those girls would be using to re-create *THEIR* dresses, that's what worried him. How much time did it take them to make them? How much work was involved. What was it all going to cost him? Fenner's worried look prompted the sheikh to offer him a drink, which he had poured from an ornate pot on a nearby shelf. Yes, thought Fenner, a nice large whisky or brandy would go down well about now. He took the glass and swallowed its contents in one gulp, at the same time keeping his eye on *that* door where *those* girls were spending *his* money. After his mighty swallow, Fenner looked into the empty glass and asked the sheikh, 'What was that?' His curiosity whetted.

'Camels' milk,' was the reply as Fenner began to cough his way into the next world.

It was a strange feeling for Mabel, Jo-Jo and Lynn, working on their familiar workroom table at the exhibition but without the presence of Paddy, Kathy and Olive.

Their conversations were less frequent and so were their stoppages, Fenner would have been delighted had he known how well the three girls were working. Tony was cutting quite normally, and they were busy sewing quite normally. Yes, it was strange. Jo-Jo looked at her watch. 'I wonder how they're getting on?' she said.

'All right I should think,' said Lynn, really zooming along a seam.

'I expect it's nice by the river at this time of the year,' said Mabel, stroking Twinky with one foot whilst she drove her electric foot pedal full down with the other, making her machine almost run hot.

'I don't know,' queried Jo-Jo. 'You know what these foreigners are like sometimes.'

'No,' said Lynn with Mabel's concurrence. 'Well, you know, when they're away from home they go a bit mad, don't they?'

'What? Drinking you mean?' said Lynn, finishing a sleeve.

'Arabs don't drink,' said Mabel wisely.

'Coo, that won't please Fenner, he likes a drop . . . if it's free,' said Jo-Jo.

'I wonder if they're having a raving party?' said Lynn naughtily.

'That sheikh is a perfect gentleman,' said Mabel firmly. 'He speaks beautifully.'

'What's that got to do with it?' asked Lynn.

'Nothing,' butted in Jo-Jo.

'Why, it shows breeding,' said Mabel proudly.

'You're right there,' said Tony, overhearing. 'With about ten wives, they breed all right.'

'I can't believe that,' said Mabel doubtfully.

'What? All those women, all that money and no television, what else have they got to do?'

'Coo, love in the desert,' said Lynn as she broke into part of *The Desert Song*.

'You've seen that film too many times, too much Omar Sherriff,' criticized Jo-Jo incorrectly.

'I would imagine it's very romantic,' said Mabel, mourning her missed chances.

'What?' said Jo-Jo. 'All that sand in your butter and living in tents! I had some of that last year on our camping holiday near the sea.'

'It's not like that,' said Lynn hopefully, praying her illusion wouldn't be shattered.

'Well,' said Tony, resting his scissors. 'I know what it's like riding a camel.'

'Have you been out there then?' said Lynn, searching for the truth.

'No, this was at the zoo last year!'

Lynn's romanticism crumbled, thinking how ordinary they made it sound.

The floating harem on *Checkmate* was even more sumptuously adorned than the sheikh's main cabin. Everything in the harem was wispy and delicate, even the cushions that lay around were gaily embroidered with finely intricate silk work. The 'room' was not as well lit as the other cabin, since the porthole windows were screened by soft luxurious curtains and laces, and the whole atmosphere was seductive. A heavy eastern perfume filled the air which gave everything a sleepy feeling, one of peace and serenity, lulled even more by the tinkling ornaments suspended all around, sounding tiny chimes to the movement of the boat in the water. The whole room was completely feminine, and the girls from Fenner Fashions loved every womanly piece of it. There were three harem girls: Jasmin the youngest at about eighteen; and the two other girls were about twenty and twenty-four respectively. The oldest girl seemed to be in charge, for it was she who ushered out Abdul the bodyguard, and welcomed Paddy, Kathy and Olive to their own personal domain. She introduced herself as Sahleet and the other girl as Camilla. She struggled with 'Paddy' but managed Kathy and Olive upon their reciprocal introductions.

The harem girls spoke very little English, though Jasmin spoke more than the other two, quite good French, but not a word of Cockney. However, the language of women was seemingly international when it came to clothes. In order to demonstrate what needed to be done to take measurements for fittings, etc., Paddy realized that the best way was to demonstrate by example. She got Kathy and Olive, her two 'models', to peel off their clothes while she took their measurements. The harem girls watched with interested astonishment as Kathy and Olive revealed what western women wore 'underneath'. With sign language and spot drawings the two cultures were able somehow to converse with each other. It seemed that Jasmin, Sahleet and Camilla couldn't understand why western women wore their prettiest clothes 'underneath'. Why wear any clothes underneath at all if no one was going to see and admire them? This led to much giggling between Paddy and the girls of Fenner Fashions as their imagination turned to conversation.

'I can imagine Fenner's face if we all rolled up for work in our bras and pants,' said Paddy.

'I can imagine his mind,' said Kathy.

'What about getting on the bus?' thought Olive, laughing.

'What about going upstairs?' said Paddy rolling with laughter.

'My bum wouldn't half wobble,' said Olive a bit embarrassed.

'Yours would?' screamed Kathy. 'What about Jo-Jo's?'

'I reckon it would dance,' roared Olive.

'Dance!' howled Paddy. 'Talk about the black bottom.'

The three Fenner girls were falling all over the place with laughter, and it was impossible to explain to the three Arab girls what it was all about, but fortunately, their laughter was so infectious the Arab girls laughed too.

The fun of the situation continued. The laughing broke out again when Kathy said how funny it would be if men wore only their underclothes. 'Especially old Fenner!'

'Yes,' laughed Paddy. 'He wears those peek-a-boo shorts.'

This time Paddy was able to explain to Jasmin what they were laughing about. The Arab girls howled with laughter but quickly fell into near silence for they were laughing about men, 'their lords and masters', but it was all so funny they just had to muffle their laughter in the thick 'soundproof' cushions.

The giggling and laughing got worse when Paddy found that they thought Paddy had meant men going around in women's underwear and not, as Paddy had tried to explain, in their own.

A new wave of fantasies rolled from their imaginations as they visualized their respective menfolk in knickers and bras. Of course, Fenner sprang to the forefront for the butt end of the jokes.

'Just think,' said Paddy. 'Here's Mrs Fenner always thinking he's going around with other women . . .'

'Yes,' jumped in Kathy, 'if she caught him in women's underwear she'd think he was going around with a fella.'

'Ooh,' said Olive. 'I can't imagine my Arthur in knickers and a bra, I mean he works in the docks.'

'I doubt whether my boyfriend would keep 'em on,' said Kathy, giggling at the thought.

'Why's that?' asked Paddy.

'Well, he's always trying to get mine off.'

All the girls were laughing openly now, it was all too funny to hold back.

The deck walk had revived Fenner and the sheikh had been most helpful in his hour of need. They had rested on the deck whilst Fenner's breath had been regulated. The man fishing in a small boat on the Warsash side of the river would never know that a passenger on *Checkmate* had nearly expired, and no one supposed he'd even care for, unlike some, he sat floating on the river, completely at peace.

'The girls seem to be happy,' said the sheikh at last, noting Fenner's cheeks turning from bright blue to a pillar-box red, as the coughing fit abated.

'Yes, they do,' wheezed Fenner, his cheeks turning to a light beige yet again.

'Clothes are a common enough subject among western women. But eastern women wear much less and therefore are less affected.'

'Yes, of course,' gasped Fenner, thinking how fortunate they wore less, it wouldn't cost so much in materials. This made him feel better. He had to retain his wits about him, because he had for the first time been forced to let his girls go it alone, and God knows what they would get up to, he thought. He had always been able to supervise all the materials and costs in the past, but now a more difficult problem lay before him, especially after he had given a price to the sheikh. This had been exorbitant, allowing for his on-the-the-spot guessing at cost of materials and labour and a little bit for unseen circumstances, but now the reins were taken out of his hands, a different complexion had been thrown on things entirely. He somehow had to get with those girls, to supervise them.

As Paddy, Kathy and Olive measured and fitted the harem girls, they talked about the different lives they led. Jasmin translated on behalf of Sahleet and Camilla, who were amazed and sometimes shocked at the differences in life-style between them and the factory girls.

'Ees Meester Fenner your eunuch?' asked Jasmin in broken English.

This started the girls laughing.

'Yes,' answered Paddy, laughing. 'In a way I suppose he is.'

'He guards you against intruders?'

'That's right,' said Kathy, 'he won't let the customers near us in case we find out what he's charging for our work.'

'And are you hees women?'

'Oh yes,' giggled Olive. 'We're all Fenner's girls.'

'And does he have a favourite?'

'Oh, no,' said Paddy. 'He has to treat us all equal.'

'Has to?'

'Oh, yes,' said Kathy. 'Union rules – he's got to.'

'What ees theese Union rules?'

'Well,' said Paddy. 'Though we're his girls, as you say, we've got rules or laws if you like, so he can't do just what he likes.' Paddy went on to put the answer in a way that Jasmin and the girls would understand. At this Jasmin jabbered rapidly to Sahleet and Camilla, whose faces showed obvious surprise at what Paddy had said.

'Do you do stitching work?' asked Jasmin prompted by Sahleet.

'Oh yes,' said Olive with Paddy and Kathy nodding in agreement.

'Do you like it?'

'No, not much,' said Kathy.

'But he forces you to do it?' suggested Jasmin eagerly.

'No, never,' said Paddy, straightening her back. 'We only do it for money.'

'He pays you for thees work?' said Jasmin excitedly.

'We wouldn't do it otherwise,' said Kathy.

Jasmin talked to the other two harem girls who sat dumbfounded as they listened to her interpret what the other girls had said.

'And what about bedroom duties?' said Jasmin gingerly.

'Oh, we've got our own man for that,' giggled Olive.

'He doesn't mind you having your own men?'

'No,' said Paddy. 'He only wants us to do the stitching.'

'For which he pays you?' Jasmin was amazed.

She reported to the other girls and the more she related the more excited they got, until their jabbering became incessant. Paddy, Kathy and Olive had told the harem girls how their working lives operated, using parts of Jasmin's meanings to fit their own. What they didn't realize was the extreme difference in the two cultures and ways of life. In the case of Fenner, for instance, Jasmin had inferred that he was a sort of sheikh and the factory girls had accepted the fact that he was, in a way. But Jasmin had interpreted it that Fenner was a sheikh in the Arabian meaning, and these were his concubines, who obviously had it very easy, being paid for their 'stitching' work and allowed to have other lovers than the sheikh. Their lives were really thousands of years of customs and evolutions apart. The Arab girls accepted their lives as they had done since time began, whereas Fenner's girls, like all Western civilizations, had progressed past white slavery and were now at the threshold of sex equality.

The girls had almost forgotten about their original reason for being there and were seated comfortably around on the splendorous cushions with Jasmin, Sahleet and Camilla, all having a good old 'chin-wag'. Kathy and Olive were still dressed in the gowns they had 'modelled' for the harem girls, and Paddy lay relaxed, smoking – with the measuring tape hanging idly round her neck.

'What are your duties?' asked Paddy.

'We rise every morning at six of the clock and face the east to Allah.'

'Six o'clock!' repeated Paddy.

'Oi, Pad,' said Olive naturally. 'That would be overtime, wouldn't it?'

'You're bloody right, it would,' said Paddy, explaining it all in detail to Jasmin who in turn translated it to Sahleet and Camilla. 'Then what?' continued Paddy.

'Well,' said Jasmin. 'We have to bathe very quickly and have a simple meal, to be ready to await our master's call should he want us.'

'That's like half hour for breakfast,' Kathy pointed out to Paddy.

'Yes, and a quarter of an hour washing hands time before that.'

Paddy explained that their master couldn't call upon them until they'd washed their hands and had their morning break.

'And that's how you say, your law?' asked Jasmin.

Paddy and the others waited till Jasmin had explained to the other harem girls what had been said, before they inquired about their other duties.

'Well,' said Jasmin. 'Some of us do our stitching work, we may have to clean our master's rooms or cook our master's meals and serve them to him.'

'Four different jobs,' said Olive.

'Precisely,' replied Paddy.

'Now then,' she said to Jasmin slowly. 'This is what would happen in our factory . . .' She cleared her throat and began. 'First of all, we only do our set jobs, we don't do other people's work that would do them out of a job.' Jasmin nodded and passed that 'snippet' on to the others. 'Secondly, each job would have a separate amount of time in which to do it and a different payment too.'

Both Kathy and Olive nodded in brotherly agreement. Sahleet and Camilla giggled at the thought of such 'carryings on' after Jasmin had explained it to them. Jasmin was getting intrigued at what appeared to her as outrageous at first, but now made mental notes of all that Paddy was telling her and didn't wait to be asked, 'What next?', but ventured on outlining in detail to Paddy what the harem girls' day consisted of. 'Of course,' she said eagerly, her English improving with use, 'we are always confined to the harem quarters and are not allowed out.'

'Oh,' said Paddy, stubbing out her cigarette to accentuate the point. 'We wouldn't have that.'

'No way,' agreed Kathy and Olive.

'Well,' said Olive. 'We'd never get our shopping done otherwise.'

Jasmin drooled at the thought of being 'let out', as she reported to the other girls.

'I can see you need a Union,' said Paddy, summing up. 'You're being exploited.'

'How could we have a Union?'

'Well, all you do is just get together and refuse to do things unless you get the things *you* want.'

Jasmin looked strangely at them.

'You know,' said Kathy with a wink. 'When the old sheikh comes in at night for his nightcap Nookie, don't let him have it.'

'Seems a shame really,' said Olive, 'giving up all that pleasure. I wish Arthur would have a few more nightcaps.'

Jasmin couldn't understand what Paddy and the girls meant at all and pressed them for an explanation.

'Blimey,' said Paddy. 'This is going to be difficult!' She looked at the three harem girls waiting in puzzled anticipation. 'What's the Arabic word for Nookie?'

'I don't know,' said Kathy with a don't-ask-me look.

'I thought it was international,' said Olive with worldly wisdom.

'It is. But they don't all call it the same as we do.'

'I know,' said Olive in a flash. 'I've got a woman's magazine in my bag.' She leaned over a cushion to reach it.

'What good's that?' asked Kathy.

'Well . . .' Olive was rapidly thumbing through the magazine pages.

'All those holiday romance stories in them serials, they don't say Nookie, they say things like making love and all that.'

'So?' said Paddy, still puzzled.

'Well, if you read the stories or bits of them, you'll see how they say it and you can use the same idea.'

Kathy and Paddy looked at Olive for a while, thinking she had proposed an Oliveism, until suddenly Paddy saw its possibilities.

'Give us that magazine,' she said, grabbing it at the place Olive had found.

The harem girls had sat in silence during this exercise to overcome the language barrier and leaned further forward as Paddy began to read. She looked at Jasmin and said, 'The sheikh? Right?' And she read on ' ". . . he crept past the Spanish waiter who was dozing on the patio after a busy day in the dining-room and, keeping in the shadows from the bright moon, made his way to her downstairs *bedroom* . . ." ' Paddy emphasized by raising her voice on the word 'bedroom', then read on ' ". . . she lay on the *bed* . . ." ' she shouted ' ". . and he approached her waiting *body* . . ." ' another shout ' ". . . he began to kiss her waiting *lips* and she *surrendered* to his *advances*." ' Paddy looked at Kathy and Olive and said excitedly, 'Here it is, here it is.' She read on ' ". . . after an eternity, they *made love* . . ." ' she shouted even louder to Jasmin ' ". . . till the early hours without a care . . ." ' She stopped, saying to Kathy, 'then it just goes on about the bloody spoil sport Spanish waiter outside on the patio'. Paddy turned to Jasmin, 'That's the sort of thing,' she said hopefully.

'Oh, is that a Union magazine?'

Paddy, Kathy and Olive fell back on the cushions in exasperation.

'No,' said Paddy, sensing failure at their efforts. 'The making love bit?' she pleaded to Jasmin.

'Yes, I understood that. But I thought you were wanting me to know about a Spanish waiter.'

'Oh Gawd,' said Paddy, laughing. 'The making love bit, you understand what I mean?'

'Of course. Our master comes to his harem and picks his fancy and they make love. It's as simple as that.'

Paddy sat up straight. 'That's exactly what I mean. When the sheikh comes in at night, whoever he picks, don't let him have it.'

'You mean deny the master his rights?' gasped Jasmin in horror, not even daring to translate such blasphemy to her colleagues.

'Yes,' said Paddy emphatically. 'Stop his rights to get your rights.'

Whilst Jasmin lengthily conveyed the translation to Sahleet and Camilla, Paddy and the girls flopped back on the cushions exhausted.

'And that's how we get a Union?' said Jasmin finally.

'Yes,' said Paddy definitely.

The luxury of the harem was filled with deep thought.

The sheikh, having been called to the bridge of the yacht to take a long distance call, afforded Fenner the opportunity he'd been waiting for to spy on the girls. He had climbed on to the top sun deck and seeing a half-open skylight he peered in. The girls were draping the semi-nude Arab girls in the new creations and pinning them into place. The sight of the semi-naked harem divorced his intentions from their true course, for with so much 'boob and bum' to look at he completely forgot about the cost of the new gowns. Shuffling about to improve his view, he leaned further over the skylight. It never struck him that he was in fact a 'peeping Harold'. The lusciousness of the young girls filled his entire mind with thoughts about the types of girls he would have in his own harem, when he collected his fortune – which was close at hand. Also close at hand, though unseen, were several of the yacht's crew who were busily renewing a rope for hoisting the yacht's navigational lights through a mast-head pulley. This meant nothing to Fenner as he gazed on far more interesting shapes than a coil of white rope, but the end of the rope did – for it was looped round Fenner's foot. The sailors, in their endeavours to pull the long rope to its restay place, gave it an extra strong tug when they felt resistance to the rope's previously easy going run. That had been Fenner's weight, which was easily catapulted through the open skylight by a three-sailor-powered pull.

The screams of, 'Rape', 'Murder', 'Bloody Hell', 'Allah', and 'Infidel', complete with some Arabic versions of the same words were heard throughout the entire length and breadth of *Checkmate*, including the top of the flagpole where a perching seagull wheeled over the sleepy Hamble village, screeching, 'Rape, murder, police . . .' to other English screeching seagulls. Abdul's sixteen stone moved quicker than a nudist who'd spilt a cup of hot chocolate in his lap, and was first to arrive on the scene. Fenner had landed on the cushions among all the nudes, and was busily pushing away boobs and bums in order to breathe.

The arm lock that Abdul placed around Fenner's neck began to have an effect in as much as it brought back the old complaint that he had suffered recently on the yacht. Two severe attacks of loss of breath.

The light blue colour of his coughing fits was returning to his face and his tongue complimented the light blue with a dark mauve. The girls, meanwhile, had covered themselves with garments hurriedly clutched to their naked bosoms. The arrival of the sheikh saved Fenner's life. Abdul released his stranglehold on orders from the sheikh who began thumping Fenner's back to help the recommencement of his lung action. Choking and gasping, Fenner was, for the third time, assisted out on to the deck by the sheikh and Abdul, having made the round trip in a little short of four and a half minutes. The pandemonium that Fenner's fall had caused had already abated in the harem.

'Coo,' said Paddy. 'Old Fenner's gone through the roof a few times but never from the outside!' She giggled.

'Serves him right,' said Kathy callously. 'He was having a crafty butchers at the birds' bodies.'

'I didn't think he was like that,' said Olive.

'All men are,' Kathy generalized with a sweep of her arms that encompassed the world's male population, and an oil rig in the North Sea.

'No,' said Paddy with authority. 'I know what he was up to. He was seeing how much material we'd use and how long we'd take to fit it.'

'Yes, that's more like it,' Olive agreed.

Paddy and the others completed the dress fittings, collected their belongings and bid their farewells. Jasmin was sorry to see them go, as were Sahleet and Camilla, but the hug that Jasmin gave Paddy was the firmest of all. It was a hug of enlightenment and introduction into Women's Lib and sex equality, though Paddy thought it was just the hug of sincerity.

'Yes,' Fenner was saying to the sheikh. 'I was just walking round and admiring your yacht, when I tripped and fell through the skylight.'

'Allah be praised that you had a soft landing. The cushions are of the finest quality and designed to afford every comfort with their soft filling.'

'Yes,' said Fenner, remembering that it had really been three pairs of boobs and bums that had broken his fall, though he dare not tell the sheikh. Noticing the beady look in Abdul's eyes, he didn't have to tell him.

'No matter,' continued the sheikh. 'I am delighted with my gains, I have a fine wardrobe for my girls and Kathy and Olive will be a fine addition to my harem.'

Paddy, Kathy and Olive stepped out on to the deck just in time to hear the end of the sentence.

'What does he mean? Olive and me will be a fine addition to his harem,' said Kathy to Paddy.

'I'm not sure,' said Paddy, thinking. 'But I wouldn't mind betting Fenner's charged such a high price for our dresses, the sheikh probably thinks he's bought you two as well.'

'That bloody white slaver,' said Kathy fuming. 'I bet Fenner put him up to it.'

'If anybody's a white slaver, it's Fenner,' snapped Paddy. 'He proves it every day in the factory.'

'What are we going to do?' asked Kathy.

'Will you have to work out the rate?' Olive asked Paddy, not quite sure what was going on.

Paddy and Kathy looked at her in amazement. 'Yes,' Paddy laughed. 'And we'll both live on your immoral earnings.'

Meanwhile, Fenner had adopted a piece of north country wisdom. When in doubt, say nought. He found himself in a crossfire. He didn't want to upset the sheikh and his sales order and he didn't want the girls to know anything about his dealing methods. He was quite prepared to let the sheikh think what he liked as long as he paid for his purchases. Unfortunately, for him, he'd seen the girls come on to the deck from the saloon, and knew they'd overheard what concerned the purchase of Olive and Kathy.

The girls' plan was much simpler than Fenner's. Get off the yacht! So, with that in mind, they made their way to the gang-plank which led from the yacht to the shore and sanctuary, nodding affectionate farewells as they passed the sheikh. Abdul's bulk filled their exit route.

'Ye're all finished, Mr Fenner,' said Paddy bravely as she attempted to leave, Kathy and Olive cowering behind her. Normally the girls would have been able to handle Fenner without a problem, they could have even managed the sheikh who obviously fancied Kathy and Olive, but they couldn't weigh up Abdul. He was the fly in the ointment, he was the unknown quantity which gave them a sense of fear. Was not his job to guard the harem girls, keeping them both safe from intruders coming in and them getting out? And, furthermore, were not Kathy and Olive the two new additions to the harem?

Arthur, where are you now? thought Olive. Though Arthur would have in no way been pleased to face the Goliath Abdul on his wife's behalf, armed only with a half drunk pint of mild and bitter, a weapon Arthur never allowed to be far from his hand.

'Ah, Oi Pad,' said the sheikh. 'You are leaving us?'

'Yes please,' she answered nervously.

'Yes, and I must be popping off too,' said Fenner with difficulty. Fenner, Paddy, Kathy and Olive formed a British soldiers' 'square' and, like an Oxo cube with eight legs, edged towards the gang plank.

'When we get you on our own,' said Paddy out of the corner of her mouth to Fenner, 'we are going to get you deported to Outer Mongolia for trying to sell dresses and *slaves*.'

'*If* we get out of here,' said Fenner as the 'square' inched its way nearer the towering Abdul and freedom.

'Good-bye,' said the sheikh to Fenner and Paddy then, beckoning to Kathy and Olive, 'Come my little turtle doves, let me show you round the harem.'

Kathy and Olive huddled more closely to the others.

'You're the man, Mr Fenner,' said Olive. 'You do something.'

'He's done enough,' said Paddy. 'And when I get him on the shore, I'm going to de-man him.'

'Couldn't we do that to Abdul?' said Kathy.

'Someone already has.'

'Come along now, girls,' said the impatient sheikh.

The 'square' stood before Abdul. Here was the moment of truth, what would our courageous group do now? What did the fates hold in store? It was all like an old thriller serial, where each week the hero was confronted with some impossible ugly situation, and the excited film-goers were invited to return to the cinema next week to find out how he escaped. The group would have dearly loved to come back next week to see how they did it. From the centre of the square shot a piston-like arm, the hand clutching a Co-op plastic bag. It drew the bag back and, with the force of a charging bull rhinoceros, buried the Co-op bag deep into Abdul's ample groin. The giant bent in two, clasping his abdomen, swaying unsteadily on his sandalled feet. The square shattered into four and plunged like Apollo 16 up the gang plank. Fenner was in the lead, he believed in women and children first – after him – quickly followed by Paddy, seeing her chance to commit instant murder on Fenner. Kathy and Olive followed so closely after Paddy that they looked like a blur. Bringing up the rear was Abdul, reaching out to grab Kathy and Olive. The thunder of their feet on the floating landing stage sent a wave of terrified water through the moored craft in the yacht harbour making them bounce on their anchor cables as they were hit by hurricane 'Fenner'. Snoozing yacht owners were flung from their bunks, rickety old ladies were wobbled overboard, three dogs had a fit, and a fat company director raced for the portable toilet as a distress rocket was noisily launched. The God of speedy travellers was with the runners as, round the narrow corner, Tony and the furniture van hove into sight. Fenner and the girls watched feverishly as they ran, whilst Tony turned the van round in readiness for its journey back to the exhibition. Little did he know what a welcome visitor he was. The girls leaped into the back of the van as Fenner flung himself in the driver's cab.

'Quick,' screamed Fenner. 'Let's get out of here!' The fear on Fenner's face was enough to convince Tony that they were being pursued by the monster from the deep, and when he heard the screams from the girls in the van behind, for the first time in its life the old furniture van did a 'grid' start in the Hamble Grand Prix. The drive to the exhibition cooled the travellers' terror as the vision of Abdul racing to the van before Tony got it underway faded in the girls minds.

'What did you have in that plastic bag?' Paddy asked Olive, the heroine of the rescue.

'A quart of brown ale for Arthur?' suggested Kathy.

'No, the flat iron for pressing the dresses.' Olive proudly held up the bag, as it swung menacingly to the sway of the lorry.

The girls stared at the awesome triangular shape of its contents. 'You nearly killed Abdul,' said Kathy.

'Yes,' said Paddy, wincing at the thought. 'Especially hitting him there.'

'Well,' said Olive, lowering the bag with a bang on the van floor, 'as you said he hadn't *got* any, I thought it wouldn't hurt him.'

CHAPTER SIX

Fenner sat in the driving cab in silence as they drove along Satchel Lane, a byway from Hamble village, on the road to Southampton. His mind was churning with the events of the day. He felt he had been implicated in all sorts of happenings which were not of his making. He had never suspected that the sheikh would consider the cost of the gowns he'd ordered to include the models. Had it been Paddy the sheikh had been after, he would have gladly given him a good trade discount, and thrown in his wife and mother-in-law as an added bonus. Just think, he thought, Abdul dragging his screaming wife and mother-in-law across the blazing sands to a tent a thousand miles from anybody and him.

Fenner wasn't sure if he'd rather face Abdul or Paddy, for he knew that she would blame him for all that had happened be it right or wrong.

He didn't feel like all the hassle of arguing and eventually bargaining for peace and quiet with Paddy and the girls. The sales at the exhibition so far were good and as far as he could tell, he'd been keeping his expenses to a minimum. He had phoned the bank manager and reported his sales and Mr Thickett seemed pleased. Pleased enough to allow Fenner a bit more credit on his overdraft to complete his stay at the exhibition. On the whole the girls had worked well, considering they didn't usually. He felt it must be the change of environment and working away from home that had done it. Even so, they hadn't let him get away with too much, in fact they were earning more than they did at home base. All the extras mounted up made a very good pay packet for them, but now this business with the Arab sheikh had placed a very valuable order in jeopardy. How could he calm the troubled waters? The van turned into Hamble Lane where the signpost signalled, Netley, Hedge End and Southampton. At the end of Hamble Lane, they drove past the Solent Motel, a pleasant group of buildings in a rural setting. If he contacted the sheikh by phone, safer in view of Abdul, he reasoned, he, Harold Fenner, could use all his charm to explain the situation – and retain the order. Especially if he got it all dispatched to the yacht in record time, before the sheikh had time to think much more about previous events. And by that time the exhibition would be closed and Fenner would be fast on his way out of Southampton, clutching the sheikh's money.

Fenner's thoughts had the habit of becoming fact in his mind before they had even happened. He made no leeway for the unseen or the snags but constructed his own world and lived in it. Confident in his plan, Fenner considered the next move, the big one. How could he get the girls to work like mad to complete the order in record time to fit in with his plan? There would be arguments and bargaining, and it would cost him a fortune. Everything cost Fenner a fortune, even the office tea money seemed to be so extravagant he thought he must have shares in a tea plantation in India, or wherever they made tea. He'd had visions of this huge cargo ship loaded to the gunnels with tea for Fenner Fashions. The captain of the ship and a pirate in Merchant Navy clothing, would yell from the bridge in answer to the call from the Customs launch about the cargo he carried and he would call back on a the loud hailer, 'Tea from India, bound for Fenner Fashions,' and with that the Customs Officer aboard the launch would salute, make that funny chalk mark on the ship's side as they did on one's case at the Customs at Dover. 'We'll not hold you up,' the Customs Officer would shout to the Captain. 'On your important way and God bless all who sail in Fenner Fashions.'

If Fenner had to pay the girls extra money it would be expensive, but if he put so much in a kitty for something or other it would be so much cheaper and he would know exactly how much he was spending and saving. What could he tempt the girls with? He thought hard as the outskirts of Southampton appeared before him. Perhaps he could take them all to the cinema? No, that was too ordinary. Taking them out to dinner would cost him a fortune. Ah, that's it, he thought. One of the salesmen had said, 'There's a little cabaret club in the town.' That's it, he thought, I'll put ten quid's worth of drinks in the kitty and that would give them a start, after that they could buy their own. Yes, he'd give the club a ring and he'd be sure to get a reduction for a party booking. He reasoned it was not every night someone came in and spent ten quid for a party of, let's see, yes that is, eight of them.

Fenner's scheme was laid, all he had to do now was follow it through to its successful conclusion. He felt completely better by the time the van turned into the exhibition car park. Once Harold Fenner set his mind on a plan, nothing would turn him from his path, no problem would get him down in the dumps.

'Six quid,' he screamed in disgust to the white-coated car park attendant who got him down.

'Well, I missed you yesterday, you see, so I put it all on today's bill,' he said getting Fenner down further.

'But I'm part of this exhibition,' Fenner pleaded. 'If it wasn't for people like me, there wouldn't be an exhibition.' He spluttered over the man's white coat.

'Well, not many exhibitors bring such a large van and the price is based on size. Yours takes four parking spaces,' explained the attendant, writing out the ticket.

'I think that's robbery,' objected Fenner. 'Couldn't the four cars park inside my van?'

The attendant shook his head.

'We got invited down here by Bootles – Mister Bootle, mind you,' said Fenner trying to impress the man that he was not just dealing with some stall holder. He was Fenner of Fenner Fashions and he felt the mention of Mr Bootle would show this white-coated twit that Fenner got around in high circles.

Mr Bootle, he figured, was at least the mayor or someone important in the chamber of trade for the area. The man ignored him and handed him the bill for two days' and nights' parking – six pounds. 'You should have used the free car park,' he said.

'All right, we will,' said Fenner, getting back into the cab. 'How far's that?' he slammed the van door.

'Five and a half miles down that road.'

Getting out again, Fenner paid up with what Fenner considered to be the last money he had. And now his old mother would be thrown out of the home he was paying for with this six pounds.

'Will you be here tomorrow?' asked the white-coated red-faced man.

'Yes,' admitted the dark-suited white-faced man in a rage.

Paddy, Kathy and Olive had been reunited with the other girls in the workroom at the exhibition and were very busy indeed, relating the happenings on the sheikh's yacht over the still and silent workroom machines. They sat in their usual places and had cast aside all their work on the table to give everybody a lay-out model of the yacht.

'This was the cabin where we had tea,' said Paddy, using several piles of dress material to represent the cushions upon which they had sat.

'And this was the harem,' said Kathy, as she decorated the sewing machines with tissues to represent the lush hanging curtains on the harem porthole windows. Other dress materials were piled by Olive in the centre of the mock harem to show the eager onlookers where the harem cushions were placed.

'Dirty old sod,' said Jo-Jo, upon hearing about the sheikh's groping hands.

'I wouldn't say he was old,' said Olive, smiling at the memory.

'She enjoyed it,' said Lynn, full of attention at what was being said.

'I think it's disgusting.' Mabel turned away, then turned back quickly to casually ask, 'What happened then?'

All the girls who hadn't been there leaned forward whilst those who had, draped themselves nonchalently upon their seats, enjoying the centre stage.

'Well,' began Kathy, 'his hands were everywhere, like an Arabian octopus,' she giggled.

'More like your North Sea boyfriend,' said Jo-Jo quietly.

'Shssh,' said Lynn, annoyed at the interruption.

'Oooh,' carried on Olive. 'He put his hands right up my back and stroked me.'

'Why didn't you stop the brute?' said Mabel, trying not to listen.

'I couldn't reach his hands right up my back,' protested Olive, appealing her innocence.

'Then he started to fiddle about in the front . . . you know,' said Kathy, demonstrating.

'Oh,' gasped Mabel, refusing to listen any more, but not moving from the table.

'It wasn't half hot in there,' said Olive. 'I was feeling all giddy, all my skin started to tingle.'

'And then,' carried on Kathy, as all heads turned to her, 'he began to sweat and he was gradually pushing us back on the cushions and we could feel ourselves . . . sort of going, I could feel his breath on my ear and then . . .'

The girls were at an excitement pitch, straining their ears for the next bit, when Olive said, '. . . and then Paddy came in.'

'Oh,' sighed Jo-Jo disappointed, as Mabel breathed out in relief. Sensing the disappointment, Paddy said, 'I'm sorry if I spoilt it.' There was a touch of sarcasm in her voice. 'I should have stayed outside propping up Fenner whilst you two lost your honour,' she brought the height of intense interest to a safer level.

'Coo,' said Jo-Jo, licking her dried lips. 'He's not bad looking at all really, is he?'

'I think he's smashing,' said Lynn bravely.

'What?' said Paddy. 'You would't mind being a harem girl?'

'Well,' said Lynn, thinking about it. 'A nice-looking fella and all that money.'

'Lynn, how could you?' said Mabel sweeping the 'curtains' from her machine. 'What would your mother say?'

'She'd cry every time she lit the oil stove,' butted in Kathy with a giggle.

'Oh, daft, she wouldn't,' said Lynn, wondering what her mother *would* say.

Paddy laughed at their banter. 'Oh, it's the first time I've laughed since Fenner fell through the skylight.'

'Ooh yes, tell us about that,' said Jo-Jo eagerly, wanting to hear it all again.

'Well,' began Paddy, 'we'd gone in to the harem to measure up the girls, and this Jasmin, you know the one I told you about, and her two mates Sahleet and Camilla, got stripped off for us to fit the dresses.' The girls all leaned forward again. 'Well, we were talking about our union and I was saying *they* ought to get one, they don't half have bad conditions. Well, we didn't know at the time, but old Fenner must have been spying on us from above. Well, I'd just said to Kathy, "I wonder where Fenner is," and he fell through the roof! Oh, we died of laughing,' said Paddy as they all started laughing at it again. 'And that wasn't all, he'd fallen on top of all the nude harem girls, and when that big Abdul came in, he thought old Fenner was trying to have it away with the three of them at once.'

The girls were falling all over the table laughing at the story, when Fenner came into the workroom. Paddy looked up and said, 'Shouldn't you have come through the roof, Mr Fenner?'

With that all the girls went into uncontrollable hysterics while Fenner stood there in front of them, boiling in oil.

'And what are we making dresses of now? Kleenex?' Fenner said sarcastically. 'If I paid your wages in paper money you wouldn't be very pleased would you?' he rambled on not realizing what he'd said in his anger.

The girls giggled, as they cleared the mock harem and sheikh's cabin from the work-bench.

'I was just telling the girls how you tried your hand at the white slavery business, Mr Fenner,' Paddy said with a sting.

'Now, Paddy. That's all been dealt with.' Fenner was still smarting from the lash of Paddy's tongue after they had got back from the yacht. 'Now then,' he addressed all the girls. 'I've got a nice little surprise for you all.' (He was leaving Fenner Fashions? someone hoped from the back.) 'As you have worked quite well, and some of you have had a few extra problems,' he looked at Kathy and Olive, 'I have arranged a little treat for you tonight. We are all going, or those who want to,' he put in quickly (No point in wasting money, he thought), 'to a little night club in the city here. I'm putting in a kitty for the drinks to start you off.'

'What have we got to put in?' asked Paddy suspiciously.

'You buy only the extras that you want, like meals or gambling.'

A bubble of excitement ran through the girls and Fenner beamed at their obvious pleasure.

'No,' said Paddy. 'I mean, what have we got to do in return for you?'

'Now why is it, Paddy, that every time I offer to treat everybody you always think there's an angle to it?'

'Because there always is. There is, isn't there?' she pressed.

'Well it's not what you'd call an angle,' said Fenner, cracking at the seams a little.

The girls groaned at the thought of disappointment.

'Well, out with it.' Paddy squared herself to listen.

'I thought,' Fenner began, 'if we lashed off that little Arab's order . . .'

'Little Arab's order . . .' exploded Paddy. 'Six dozen difficult different styled gowns?'

'Well, you designed 'em,' Fenner retaliated.

'Good job we did, else we'd have all been back home now.'

'All right. I just thought if we got the order finished, we'd *all* get our money, and as a little incentive I thought I'd sort of throw a little party, that's all.'

The girls thought it sounded reasonable and mumbled to that effect.

'If we finished an order like that we would earn a lot of bonus, wouldn't we?' said Paddy, not so easily swayed as the others.

'Of course.'

'Then what you're offering is a little party on top of that?' said Paddy.

'Precisely,' said Fenner firmly.

Paddy felt there was a catch in it somewhere but she couldn't see one yet. 'We don't have to go on that sex maniac's yacht?'

'No,' said Fenner equally firm.

'And you'll give us a little party tonight?'

'I said I'll get the drinks or at least start you off for a . . . er couple of hours,' he said quickly, working out how much drink his girls could consume in two hours. Mabel a Guinness, Lynn an orange juice, he reckoned . . .

'OK,' said Paddy at last, to a cheer from the girls. 'We'll go after we finish tonight.'

'Good. That's arranged then. Now will you get on with your work?' he said and called for Tony.

'I don't mind going on the yacht,' said Tony.

'Get on with you,' said Fenner.

The girls settled down to their work with renewed effort.

Kathy and Olive continued to model the new creations and business was booming. The overseas visitors enjoyed and bought the new designs in good numbers, along with many other articles on show which had been brought as stock, and offered for sale with an alteration and fitting service. The area which Kathy and Olive used as a dressing-room each time they put on a show was also used by prospective customers having their new dresses fitted. This affected the banter between the girls, being free and easy among themselves, but restrained when they had visitors backstage. However, as the day progressed, the girls almost got used to having strangers walking about their domain and became more relaxed in their presence;

especially as many of them could not speak much English anyhow. Southampton, being an ocean terminal, brought many travellers passing through from all over the world. It was never unusual for the citizens of that internationally-known port to see a whole range of traditional costumes when shopping around the town. Stretching from the brightly coloured head scarves and dresses of Nigerian women to the kimonos of the Japanese, though some visitors from distant lands wore western dress and were often only recognizable by their facial features or light-weight clothes, ideal for the tropical sunshine of their native lands. Paddy, being the supervisor as well as shop steward, usually supervised the dress fittings. She could then not only keep her eye on the customers' requirements but also the girls' bonus extras from the additional work.

Kathy and Olive had now quite got the idea of modelling and Twinky enjoyed his hourly walk round the stage during the fashion shows. Tony was beside himself on the microphone and wore gaily coloured handkerchiefs and shirts on his appearances, and spoke with a more pronounced effeminate voice to add to the colour, as compère of the show. Fenner clucked around like an anxious rooster over his brood, trying to help here and there, only to be rudely told to go here or there. But he enjoyed what appeared to be the well-oiled machine of Fenner Fashions to which he had now added INTERNATIONAL on the display board. Yet another recent addition was *Suppliers of dresses to Sheikh Ali Achmud* which brought many strange stares from foreign visitors, thinking that they had either got their English wrong or that the sheikh really wore dresses. A large Australian gentleman in a bush hat had said, 'Stone the bloody crows, Bruce, that sheikh must be some sort of Arabian poof!' Bruce nodded in agreement at the blunt comment, whilst a more timid Italian couple searched through their Italian/English – English/Italian phrase book but were unable to find an appropriate word that would describe the sheikh. There didn't seem to be a 'la Poofo' in the book anywhere, so Signor and Signora Gadaselli crossed themselves in reverence and walked on. A bishop from somewhere or other, on the other hand, looked down at his own flowing robes and, with a red face to match, gathered them up from his feet and glided away, giving everybody a flash of a well-turned ankle. Frau Haunfstiegal was quite a large lady, well, perhaps a bit bigger than large, rather getting on for enormous, without being downright fat. This, however, had nothing to do with her good German sense, for she could see that, clad in the wrap-around gown of Fenner Fashions International, much of her ampleness would be cunningly concealed. She was welcomed into the 'tent' by a fussing Fenner who greeted her with a '*Bonjour, signor*' – his best French and Italian.

He bustled this ample piece of export income towards the fitting-room with all the charm imaginable, not forgetting to tell Frau Haunfstiegal that he owned all this, as far as the eye could see. She lifted her spectacles to view the distant domain, and lowered them to assist her short-sightedness to focus on the extent of his kingdom, a few yards away. The 'commander' strode on past his 'troops' busy at their machines, giving them a wave of authority, until he reached the fitting-room, where he was greeted with an arm thrust through the curtains and into his chest.

' 'Op it,' said the voice of Paddy.

Fenner stumbled at the obstacle and looked sheepish, for the commander had tripped over his sword.

Frau Haunfstiegal entered the 'temple' and was greeted by the high priestess of fashion.

'Hello,' said Paddy, viewing the bulky Frau and wondering if they'd brought enough material from London to fit her.

'*Morgen,*' said the Frau with Teutonic curtness. She would have been an active forty-eight or -nine years of age, neat and proper in her appearance and very confident in her bearing. This, of course, made no difference to Paddy, who treated all and sundry with a basic indifference. With hand signals and grunts, Paddy ordered the Frau to disrobe, gesticulating with a tape measure. Frau Haunfstiegal, looked around her for signs of any male eyes that might be in the vicinity. Crossing to the curtains, she closed a tiny gap which overlooked the workroom. Having checked all the security arrangements, she struggled with her fat arms to reach the zip at the back of her dress. She grunted and groaned as she fought to unzip it, like an overgrown 'porker' trying to extricate a flea from an awkward place with its trotter. Paddy stood watching and waiting, listening to the straining harness of her underwear as it creaked like a rider adjusting his seat on a new leather saddle. Finally, the noisy whirr of the zip indicated that it was undone, and the wrestling movements of Frau Haunfstiegal wriggling out of her dress, reminded her of an escape artist in the final throes of freeing himself from the stiff canvas strait-jacket, to a roar of applause from the cinema queue. The Frau's heavy underwear held her in reasonable shape, though she spilled over at various places above the pink elasticated bra and girdle. Her suspender belt looked more like an officer's 'Sam Brown', designed for supporting sword and pistol, rather than the delicate silk stockings that clung on the end of them, like over-filled net shopping bags. Paddy gazed upon the awesome sight of the semi-nude Frau, terrified of something bursting and killing her stone dead.

Then she looked at the stool upon which she invited the Frau to stand in order to take her measurements. Paddy visualized the stool either splaying its legs like a foal's first collapsing attempts at walking or simply sinking into the solid wooden floor of the exhibition hall, piercing the polished surface with its legs in four places.

Frau Haunfstiegal mounted the stool and groaned as she did, so did the stool. Accepting a supporting hand from Paddy with a short, '*Danke*,' she wobbled her way to an upright position and stood erect like a huge Venus de Milo, with arms, on a wooden plinth. Paddy began to measure the Frau with the tape measure that seemed to be far too short, and was forced to enlist her aid to hold it against herself whilst Paddy took a few more steps to circumnavigate her girth to complete the measurement. The hand signals from the two women assisted the operation. Paddy, asking the Frau in English, 'Lift up your arm, please,' and demonstrating with her arm what she required the Frau to do.

The stand next to Fenner Fashions displayed jewellery, expensive jewellery. Its length ran the full length of Fenner's stand, having on view to passing visitors a large collection of photographs showing some of the jewellery offered for sale. The visitors, rich or curious enough to be further interested, were invited to the back of the stand where they would sit upon comfortable armchairs and chaise-longues, while the sales people brought out from a huge safe at the back of the stand, trays of valuable and sparkling ornaments in exotic shapes, forming necklaces, bracelets, pendants, ear-rings, tiaras and so on. Even the smart red leather boxes they came in, according to

Fenner, would 'cost a fortune'. In addition to the crowd of visitors and sales people, there were at least half a dozen security men and women on hand to guard the treasures. Fenner hated the stand and what it represented, for any time his wife got near such a place it usually ended in 'costing him a fortune'. The only good thing about it was that it drew a lot of people to their part of the exhibition and it looked good for Fenner Fashions to be in such rich and exquisite company who were not in competition with him.

'Do you like green?' said Paddy to the balancing Frau.

'Green?' she queried in mimicking English.

'Yes . . . er . . . *Ya,*' said Paddy having a shot at German.

'Vos is das?' said Frau Haunfstiegal confusing the issue.

'Green!' said Paddy guessing her request. 'Green,' she repeated indicating the floor and mimicking a lawn-mowing action.

The Frau, thinking Paddy had meant she should be rolled out flatter like pastry, shook her head in disgust. '*Nein, nein,*' she said.

In despair Paddy tried another colour. 'Blue?' she suggested. 'Blue?' she repeated and pointed to the sky.

The Frau looked up and saw the dirty grey of the ceiling, tarnished by the smoke of a million cigarettes, cigars and pipes from all the smokers that had attended thousands of functions in the hall. Frau Haunfstiegal was not wearing Battleship Grey.

By holding up samples of different coloured cloths, Paddy was able to establish the colour and type of material, Frau Haunfstiegal chose to beautify herself in. Having settled on that, Paddy enlisted Kathy to help her assemble the new gown around the Frau's barrel-like form. The girls wrapped and pinned what seemed like several miles of material round the Frau before most of the rolling pink flesh was hidden.

Kathy giggled to Paddy, 'Christ, she's got more wrapping round her than that Egyptian mummy, Toots and Carmen!' she mispronounced it, knowing Frau Haunfstiegal couldn't understand.

'Never mind about that,' said Paddy, watching a pin bend against the strain. 'The more material, the more bonus.'

'If we get many more like her, we'll need another load of cloth,' said Kathy, forcing her fingers between flesh and material to insert a stronger pin. 'I shouldn't fancy carrying her over the threshold,' she said in a matrimonial vein.

'All right, if she married someone like big Abdul.' Paddy stood back to view the finished job as Kathy held the full-length mirror for the Frau to inspect her own 'mummification'.

'Ya – is good,' said the Frau, admiring herself in the mirror.

'Another satisfied bonus,' quipped Paddy and she and Kathy started to remove the gown for it to be sewn in the workroom.

Olive, in preparation for the next fashion show, entered the fitting-room where Frau Haunfstiegal was being disrobed. 'Nearly time,' she said to Kathy, dragging Twinky in behind her on his lead.

'Just done,' said Kathy as she took hold of one end of the material wrapped round the Frau. Twinky was not a dog to be sported with, he didn't enjoy being pulled around by Olive in the changing-room. He either wanted to get out for a run on the stage, or return to his molly-coddling mistress, Mabel, in the workroom. Either way, he pulled his lead taut as Olive held him. Kathy, a heavy but more shapely girl than Frau Haunfstiegal, hit the taut dog's lead at about calf level and she fell, like the Pisa Tower finally deciding to lean too far at last, gripping the only thing she had in her hands for support, the material wrapped around the Frau, she pulled as she fell. Frau Haunfstiegal spun on the small stool like the White Tornado for a split second, and as she gained momentum, she rose into the warm air and whirl-winded her way through the curtains right into the Jewellery Showroom next door.

The salesman who began to fasten an expensive necklace round the neck of a seated lady buyer, never expected to be hit in the back by a flying nude 'Good Year Blimp', but he was. Frau Haunfstiegal's weight against the salesman's back had forced the expensive, strong loop of necklace he was about to secure firmly around his lady customer's neck, garroting her in the true Spanish Inquisition style, though with a force normally reserved for bull elephants. Screams and gasps went up from all who were gathered in the jewellery stand, broken only by surprised laughter from Paddy, Kathy and Olive, who peered through the hole in the curtains through which Frau Haunfstiegal had disappeared. The run of bad luck began to set in for Fenner when he was summoned to Mr Bootle's temporary office in the exhibition hall. It was rather bare and divided into two rooms; one a general office that housed two typists, one young woman and an elder one, who sat at tables instead of desks, and the other office which was furnished with a small desk behind which sat Mr Bootle. There was one other chair, a hard straight-backed one in front of the desk, and the only other furnishing was an old hat stand from which hung an umbrella and a bowler hat. Mr Bootle was one of the old school of shop owners, and though he was known as Mr Bootle junior, his fifty years left the 'junior' part in doubt. He had inherited Bootles from his father and so on back through the ages to Sirus Bootle, who had started it all by selling buttons and specially treated cotton that would rot away when exposed to the air – that's why it was called Bootle's Wrapped Cotton, because it had to be kept wrapped in greased papers. He had started on a stall in a market place and made a fortune from then on, selling and replacing buttons that had been lost. All due to his rotten cotton! The fiddle upon which Bootles had been founded had long been buried in the annals of the store's history as had been the strange death of Sirus years ago, leaving a wife and several children. The booming Sirus had been found out and his swindle unearthed by the police, and Sirus had tried to hang himself but the rope broke. It was as rotten as his cotton. However, fate played an ugly trick on Sirus, because as the rope broke, he fell into a vat of boiling greased paper and was poached to death.

'Mr Fenner to see you, sir,' said the typist junior to Mr Bootle Junior, then closed the door after Fenner had entered, with a giggle.

'Take a seat, Mr Fenner,' said Bootle. Fenner looked around him, then sat on the only chair available.

'Thank you,' he said.

'I'll get straight to the point,' said Bootle through his long nose.

I think I've sat on it, thought Fenner, as the hard chair bit into his bum.

'I've had so many complaints directed against you and your employees, Mr Fenner, that I have got to consider drastic action.'

'If it's about that little problem with fuses . . .'

'Little trouble!' snorted Bootle. 'You put half of Southampton in darkness.'

'It was only a tiny fuse on the girls' Teasmade,' pleaded Fenner.

'That may be so, but the water from the explosion seeped through the wooden floor of the hall and fused a main cable.'

'Funny, the tea wasn't that strong.'

'Water fuses, Mr Fenner, not tea. Apart from that, there was the strike in our restaurant over your girls' behaviour, then the dent in the Mayor's car whilst he was opening the exhibition. Where your man was trying to park that monstrous van of yours I don't know. And on top of that, your girls fighting in the pub across the road from here.'

Fenner sat in silence as Bootle listed the other complaints through his nose. He droned on: the record player; the girls' swearing; the car park attendant; and not forgetting Frau Haunfstiegal.

'Well,' protested Fenner. 'I did offer her the dress cheap.'

'Two per cent off, *if* she took two dresses was slim compensation for that lady's embarrassment. No, I'm sorry, Mr Fenner, this has got to stop. If I'd have known all this would happen when we sent the invitation letter . . .' he moaned.

'I know,' jumped in Fenner. 'You wouldn't have let us come to the exhibition.'

'I wouldn't have had the *bloody* exhibition,' blurted Bootle, screaming his first 'bloody' in twenty years. 'I'll be quite blunt, Mr Fenner,' more bluntly than he thought he could be. 'If there is one more tiny complaint against you, your girls, Fenner Fashions in general or that blasted Twinky in particular, I shall ask you to pack up and return to London immediately.'

Fenner's personal gold standard dropped four points.

'Who?' said an Abdul-sized dress-suited man in the dimly-lit entrance of The Spanish Main nightclub.

'Fenner Fashions,' repeated Fenner. 'I telephoned.'

'Hold on,' said the doorman, using an internal phone which hardly fitted close enough to his cauliflower ear. 'Oh, yes,' he said finally, 'eight of you.' He allowed them to pass through the well-guarded portal to the cloakroom area. The old lady who took their coats hung them up on the clothes racks behind her small counter. As the girls moved into the clubroom, the old lady gave a toothless grin and pushed the 'tip' plate towards Fenner who had left to follow the others. Her smile turned to a sneer when Fenner rattled the tips plate as he dropped in a copper coloured coin into the middle of a pile of bright shining silver coins. But he rewarded the old lady with a gold-toothed smile and followed the others into the clubroom.

The decor was that of olden-day pirates, presumably of the Spanish Main era. The room blossomed out from the entrance to a balcony which had tables to sit at and look down on to the small dance floor below. At the far end of the balcony was a gambling area with a roulette wheel at its centre. Stairs led from the balcony down to the dance floor where a three-piece band played, the musicians dressed in pirates' clothes. Drinks were served at the balcony tables by waitresses in mini-skirted pirate dresses. Cutlasses and pistols of a bygone age hung around the walls and large pieces of ships masts leaned across the dance floor from the balcony, adorned with small sections of sail and rigging. Effigies and wax-faced models of fearsome pirates stood life-like in odd corners – on the balcony, up the masts, and in front of the bandstand hidden among the 'rum' barrels, which gave the impression of the quayside one would view from the deck of a ship, represented by the balcony above.

They were shown to a reserved table by a pirate girl waitress and sat themselves down. The waitress took their drinks order and left them to gaze around the crowded club. The girls had dressed themselves in the most suitable clothes they had brought with them. Each one looked very attractive in their well-fitted clothes. Well fitted because they had spent most of the day at the exhibition fitting themselves instead of Fenner's customers. Summer frocks had been 'eveningized'; trouser suits had been made more elegant and several pretty neck scarves and light-weight stoles looked remarkably like Fenner's own special material. The girls had relied on the darkly lit club to hide the material from Fenner's notice.

'Coo, this looks a posh place,' said Olive, peering into semi-darkness at some of the other long-gowned ladies.

'Very soup and fish,' said Paddy, eyeing some of the dress-suited males at the gaming table.

'I bet there's a lot of those yacht owners here,' said Kathy smiling at one, who was really a lorry driver.

'Do you go to many places like this, Mr Fenner?' asked Lynn.

'Oh, yes,' said Fenner with a voice of experience. 'Spend half my life in them,' he boasted.

'All on our hard earned money,' whispered Jo-Jo to Mabel who was nursing Twinky, wearing a black sequined collar around its neck.

'I know Mrs Fenner likes nightclubs,' said Paddy politely.

'Yes,' said Fenner regretfully, thinking that his wife's insisted visits to nightclubs had 'cost him a fortune'.

There was not much conversation from anybody, as they were all busy with their own thoughts about their new surroundings. Some of the girls were admiring the dresses of the other ladies in the club, some were admiring some of the men. Fenner was studying the lady gown-wearers, pining for the day when every woman everywhere would be wearing a Fenner creation. Inexpensive material, little stitching and machine work, cheap to make, but expensive to buy, like a Mao-Tse Tung suit for women.

Tony on the other hand was more interested in what went into the dress than the dress itself. He was a great admirer of women. He'd climb on top of any piano to get a better look down a plunging neckline. His eyes hopped from boobs to boobs as he scanned the room, enjoying it most when the band played, for then he had a grandstand view from the balcony of all the lady dancers' plunging necklines.

Mabel, on the other hand, had very different views about nightclubs and the people who frequented them. She cast her eyes round the gambling area. He's a diamond smuggler, she thought of one. She's a gunman's moll, she thought of another. In Mabel's eyes the place was full of all the characters from *The Saint* stories, undercover policemen, burglars mixing with the rich to see what jewellery they had worth stealing, gangsters passing orders to their henchmen about the next consignment of gold bullion due to arrive, and of course no self-respecting club would be complete without a rich playboy who was really a master spy. She eyed one man and decided he was the spy – actually his name was Bill Smith and he worked in an office.

The waitress arrived with a large tray of drinks. In turn she asked what they had ordered and then began to serve them. Fenner hadn't been paying much attention to the orders as they gave them quietly to the waitress on their arrival. He had been too busy looking round the club at the dresses, whilst the girls, quiet, coy and a little shy, being in such a place, had kept their voices low upon ordering them. Had they spoken at their normal level, the entire staff and customers would have heard. So it was Fenner's imagination at work as the waitress began to serve the drinks. The waitress asked Mabel. Lemonade, thought Fenner. 'Lemonade,' said Mabel and the waitress served her. Fenner smiled at his guess. Next came Lynn, Fenner smiled to himself sweetly and thought, Coca Cola. 'Vodka and lime,' said Lyn as Fenner's face dropped. Sherry, he thought for Jo-Jo. 'Rum and coke,' she said and the waitress served her. Olive, a Guinness, he thought, the waitress served her a Scotch and American.

'Gin and tonic,' said Kathy.

'Advocat,' said Paddy.

Fenner glared at Tony. 'Pint of bitter,' . . . Fenner smiled. '. . . and a whisky chaser,' added Tony to Fenner's horror.

The waitress gave Fenner a Mackeson, followed by the bill, and stood waiting for the money. Fenner smiled, thinking he'd make up the cost on the dress production and placed a five pound note on the waitress's tray. She fumbled with the change under a cloth napkin on the tray, folded the napkin over the money leaving the change on top of it. Fenner leaned over to pick up the change. The Queen's head shone brightly on the ten pence piece, which had fallen out on to his lap.

'Ten pence change out of a fiver,' he wailed.

'Cover charge on the first drinks, sir,' said the waitress bowing low over Fenner to give him a glimpse of boob.

'You'd better keep that,' he said in disgust.

The waitress stalked away also in disgust, thinking a glimpse of her boob was worth more than ten pence.

Several rounds later, the drinks cheaper after the initial cover charge had been paid, the band grew more lively and the girls feet began to tap to the music.

Another round of drinks and Paddy said, 'Oh, come on, Kath, let's have a dance.' They got to their feet and made their way down the stairs to the dance floor, followed by Jo-Jo and Olive. Lynn accepted an invitation from Tony, which left Mabel and Fenner alone at the table. Finally, Fenner asked Mabel to dance and the two of them took to the floor, dancing far enough apart to allow Twinky to breathe between them. The band, delighted that they had almost a floor full of dancers, kept playing dance after dance. Quick-steps, waltzes, foxtrots, jive, tangos and smoochers all in a varied pot pourri of music. The Fenner group on the floor danced every dance, the drinks in their tummies had become cocktails and loosened their tensions as they gaily pranced around the floor enjoying the frivolities, the Gay Gordons became a pinnacle of their exuberance and the shrieks from the dancers added to the gaiety; even Twinky yapped his approval.

After several drinks, the Fenner party had got the 'taste' and were frequent visitors to the dance floor as the tempo of their evening increased. At Fenner's place at the table, a neat little pile of drinks bills were mounting, and concealed under an ashtray to prevent them blowing away. The girls' return to the table after their lively activities on the floor was always followed by excited conversation.

' 'Ere,' said Olive after an exhausting dance, 'that fella's been chatting me up.'

'What's wrong with that?' said Jo-Jo.

'Well, he asked me to dance,' said Olive, sipping her iced drink, 'we hadn't gone four steps and he asked if he could take me home. I told him I was a married woman.'

'Did that put him off?' said Lynn, kicking off one of her shoes under the table.

'No, he was more keen. He said, "you'll know all about it then." '

The girls laughed at what Arthur might have said had he been there.

'That fella with me,' said Kathy breathlessly, 'didn't say a word, all the time we were dancing.'

'Oh,' said Paddy, 'The strong silent type, eh?'

'He was strong all right,' said Kathy. 'I could feel my bra straps breaking.'

'He'd have said something then?' suggested Olive.

'Like another dance?' said Tony to Lynn, who quickly searched under the table for her shoe with her foot and slipped it on.

'Love to,' she said, accompanying Tony to the dance floor.

' 'Ere,' said Paddy, looking at the departing couple, 'that's not a budding romance is it?'

'Ah, wouldn't that be nice,' said Jo-Jo to Mabel who thought bra strap breaking was immoral.

'They haven't been introduced,' said Mabel, speaking of a yesteryear nicety.

'No, they've only been working together for two years,' said Paddy sarcastically.

'We must get them to meet each other,' Kathy told Paddy.

'Where's Fenner gone?' said Kathy looking round the club for him.

The girls all turned but couldn't spot him, when suddenly Jo-Jo said, 'Ooh, there he is – at the gambling table.'

'Trying to win our wages,' suggested Kathy.

'As long as he's not losing them,' said Paddy threateningly.

'I'm going to have a flutter,' said Jo-Jo. 'Come on, Mabel.'

The two women and the dog moved over to the gambling table as Jo-Jo searched in her handbag for her money. Fenner stood at one end of the green baized gambling board fingering a handful of coloured chips as he watched his fortunes wane at the spin of the roulette wheel. The girls stood opposite Fenner, also watching the spinning wheel in the centre. The bets were laid and the croupier said that funny little French phrase, which meant, 'If anybody bets as the wheel stops revolving, we'll break your legs.' Jo-Jo placed her bet as the wheel stopped revolving and the croupier shot her a glance of death, but it changed to a smile when he realized her ten pence chip wouldn't break the bank and flicked it off. Fenner's luck was going badly. Having placed a large stake on number seventeen, he watched intently as, to his pleasure, the ball in the centre of the roulette wheel fell into number seventeen. A greyish-looking poodle trotted the full length of the table scattering the chips as it ran.

'No bet,' said an indignant croupier, poling Twinky away with his cane of office.

A sequinned arm reached through the crowd at the table and Twinky made a speedy exit off the table – backwards. Fenner peered at the other end of the table to lay a curse on Mabel's head, but all he heard was a yap in the crowd.

Jo-Jo had persevered and slowly lost her money when, in a brain wave, she got Twinky to lick kiss the pound chip for luck and put it on number six, the number of girls at Fenner Fashions. The wheel spun after the croupier said his little French piece, and the ball pinged and ponged round the spinning-wheel.

'Numero Sees,' called the croupier in bad French. 'Black,' he continued in English, not knowing the bad French equivalent.

'Thirty-three quid,' squealed an excited Jo-Jo to the others as she and Mabel joined them at the table.

'Most of that's my losings,' moaned Fenner, sipping his Mackey without noticing the pile of mounting bills. The girls ignored him as usual and applauded Jo-Jo as she counted her winnings.

'Well, Twinky did it,' she said. 'He kissed it for luck.'

'Typical workers' dog,' thought Fenner. 'When it saw my number coming up it robbed me.'

'Champagne all round,' said Jo-Jo to the pirate waitress. The ice bucket and tall tulip glasses all looked very impressive as they arrived at the table and the popping cork pleased everybody except the man it hit several tables away.

'To the Fenner girls,' said Jo-Jo honoured with the first toast. Several more toasts were drunk, ranging from Twinky's health, to the band who played 'Champagne Charlie is My Name', at which the entire club joined in the chorus, led by the loud Fenner girls in jubilant mood, to the delight of all the patrons of the Spanish Main which seemed to rock as it floated on the merriment. The empty champagne bottle was quickly replaced by a full one and soon the good ship 'Fenner Fashions' was sailing the Spanish Main. The light-hearted mood of everyone at the table was reflected by their antics on the dance floor, where they press-ganged other members of the clubs clientele, to give their dress-suits and long dresses an airing in the lively dances the band played for their benefit. Everybody danced with anybody that happened to be near, as the music changed tempo without stopping. The popular songs were sung, full gusto to dance steps that were invented on the spot. Soon party streamers unwound and floated on to the dancers from the balcony, shortly followed by paper hats and balloons. Lynn and Tony amid all the floor danced a cuddling smooch to anything that was played, whilst Paddy and Kathy shouted popular requests to the band, delighted at their importance. Jo-Jo in the paper garb of a pirate damsel wiggled her ample frame that would have danced in honour of Captain Morgan on his arrival in the West Indies. Olive jiggled with her tall silent admirer who now sang all the popular songs . . . in Russian. Mabel, who had completely forgotten Twinky tied to the table on the balcony, was supported by a dress-suited suitor, who whispered sweet somethings into her receptive ear. The more he whispered, the more the end of her spinsterhood seemed to hove into view. The 'conga' captivated the dancers' imagination as they followed Paddy and Fenner, who led the long snaking line of jolting conga fans throughout the club. 'Maybe it's Because I'm a Londoner' rang out through Hampshire and the shock waves of 'Knees up Mother Brown' were registered on the Reichter scale as far away as the Isle of Wight. The Spanish Main had surely sunk . . . three feet lower in the concrete water!

The 'yacht owner' that Kathy had smiled at earlier, drove them and the furniture van back to the hotel. They would never know this, but the lorry driver had all the necessary papers to drive anything, and lived a few doors away from the girls' hotel. He had delivered a heavy load for shipping to the docks that day and had stayed overnight and alone in Southampton. He had always taken his dress-suit on his long distance travels as he found visits to various night clubs more appealing to him than a drunken session in a local pub. Besides, it was better for pulling birds, as it had proved when he smiled at Kathy, sitting in the driver's cab next to him. The party was still going on in the back of the van as the revellers sang on, though no passer-by would have recognized the words. A 'Big Horse' from Fenner proved to be the song 'Because You're Mine' that he crooned to Mabel, across whose lap he lay helplessly. 'Vee rev . . . spaniel' from Paddy and Olive was not a serenade to Twinky's canine species, but a rough translation would mean, 'Up Spain' in the nicest sense, or 'Viva Espana' in the proper. Jo-Jo had gone back home for her vocal contribution and was rendering a West Indian calypso to the sleeping citizens of Southampton. 'Take Your Hand Off Me Garter' it sounded like, but any listener would have allowed much verbal leeway, thinking it must be a dialect from those distant tropical Isles. A rousing rude rugby song brought the van to the Lighthouse Hotel then burst into the night air as the volume increased when the van's doors opened and the Heavenly Choir fell out. Still floating on the drink which clouded their minds, Tony and Lynn could just be seen in the dark depths of the van, kissing and cuddling and still oblivious to the musical ride to which they had been treated. The group ('United they stood, for divided they would surely fall') waited in a singing swaying mass of paper hats and streamers to rob Kathy's new boyfriend of his recent 'pull'. Then they aimed for the stairs, and like a centipede with all its legs on one side, began to 'clonk' their way up, locked together for safety. Several snoozing guests in the other rooms were roused as the 'five pianos', or so it seemed, were hauled to the roof, hitting every stair with a thump. The renditions of the 'piano shifters' reflected the mood of the closing evening, songs of remorse and sadness were giggled in the thinning air of the building's height. The leader of the Fenner Exhibition to the top of Mount 'Lighthouse' collapsed in a heap upon reaching the summit, other members collapsed on top of him in sympathy. Tony and Lynn who had to tear themselves apart from warm embraces, were the only ones capable of helping the leader and his fallen comrades. The bulks of Jo-Jo and Kathy were rolled to their beds and Olive and Mabel clung for dear life to Twinky's lead to save them from falling backwards down the stairs. Paddy lay across Fenner's chest asleep with a sweet contented smile on her face. The elastic of a multitude of knickers and bras 'twanged' as the wearers finally got to their beds. Tony for the first time, slept soundly in his bed alone. Fenner, he had reasoned, might forget the exorbitant drinks bill he had paid and was too peaceful to move, so he therefore left him asleep on the landing!

CHAPTER SEVEN

The little men with hammers were busy inside everybody's head in the morning, to each of them it felt as though the seven dwarfs were digging a brand new mine for Snow White piecework. 'Hi Ho, Hi Ho, It's off to Work We Go' was not sung by the mourners, as they refused floating eggs in fat, and tea so strong that it could varnish the workroom table. Alka-Seltzer sales rocketed at a chemist near the exhibition hall, and their fizz in the temporary workroom, jarred on jagged nerves. Twinky won the day by dragging Olive, with Kathy hanging on her arm, at the first fashion show of the day. Fortunately, not too many early morning shoppers required the new creations, and for the first time in his rag trade career, Fenner didn't care if they spent or not, for even the jingling of coins was more than Fenner could stand in his thumping head. Tony on the other hand, directed his compèring in Romeo style to his Juliet in Lynn's clothing, 'in her workroom balcony'. The other girls moved zombie-like. Those who had to, went about their individual tasks. Paddy had decided to resign from the drinkers' union and wondered if there was a branch of Alcoholics Anonymous in Southampton. Jo-Jo, having saved her two champagne corks for luck, wondered when it would start on her aching head, whilst Mabel begged Twinky not to bark, 'Otherwise mummy will smash Twinky Winky's head in with the nearest sewing machine.'

As the morning dragged on at the pace of a ruptured tortoise, the headaches abated slightly and the need for brain surgery didn't seem to be so imperative as the Fenner Fashions glee club recovered. In fact, by about twelve o'clock and six bottles of Seltzer later, things began to get back to normal. Well, nearly normal, until the mind-blowing arrival of Jasmin at Fenner's side, claiming political asylum. Fenner had a very distinct desire to join the Foreign Legion, until he remembered that their age-old battleground was in the desert and where there were deserts, there were Arabs. He took the Foreign Legion's recruiting sergeants advice to 'Think it over, mon chère,' and decided not to enlist.

Jasmin was hustled to the workroom and out of sight of prying eyes, Abdul's eyes. She explained to Paddy and the girls that she had thought a lot of what Paddy had said to her about equality for women. So early this morning, she had dressed herself in one of Fenner's gowns, flung another piece of Fenner's material round her shoulders as a cloak, and caught the bus to Southampton from Hamble village.

'How did you pay your fare?' asked Paddy.

'I gave the conductor a ruby navel stud, and he let me ride free.'

'For the price of that,' said Paddy as the others crowded round, 'he'd have taken you to Arabia.'

'Do those buses go there?' asked Olive getting back to normal.

Nobody answered.

'You'll have to go back,' said Fenner.

'I'm claiming political asylum.'

'Then you can share my room at the asylum,' he groaned.

The girls thought for a while, staring at the lovely distressed figure of Jasmin standing before them.

'You'll just have to go back,' repeated Fenner, whose words spurred Paddy to speak.

'She can stay here.' The other girls smiled with relief.

Fenner had always thought his hearing was going, now he was sure of it. 'What?' he said in terror. 'How can she stay here?'

'Look Mr Fenner, this girl is a brother,' said Paddy firmly, as Fenner looked at the desirous form of Jasmin with curiosity on his face.

'They'd never accept her in the Boilermakers,' he laughed.

'They don't have to. She's joining our union, as a temporary brother from abroad.'

The girls applauded, and Fenner collapsed into an uncomfortable chair in the workroom.

'She is a brother in distress,' went on Paddy 'and it's our union duty to help her.'

'I can't grant political asylum,' shrieked Fenner. 'She'll have to go back.'

The shrill piercing note of Paddy's whistle, tore a hole in Fenner's Alka-Seltzered brain as she demanded, 'all out.'

The bad luck rot had again struck at Fenner's timbers, as he sensed the first cracks at his dream for riches through Fenner Fashions International start to appear. 'What about my orders?' he moaned as he gazed upon the silent sewing machines and the unstitched materials.

'I don't think you heard my orders,' said Paddy, offering the whistle to her mouth again and breathing in deeply for the blast.

'What could I do with her?' said Fenner pushing away an ugly thought from his mind.

'Employ her!'

'As what?' pushing the same evil thought away.

'As a model,' said Olive in a moment of sheer imagination.

'Yes,' said Kathy. 'Who better to model these Arabian creations than this lovely Arab girl?'

'She'd steal the show,' added Jo-Jo.

'Yes,' said Tony dreamily debating his fancy between Jasmin and Lynn.

Fenner considered for a while the prospects of stealing the show. Jasmin's beauty and carriage would certainly be an attraction, maybe, he thought, he could make a lot of money quickly and be in Peru before Abdul and the sheikh arrived. 'All right,' he agreed, realizing he needed the girls to make the lot of money he dreamed of for his fare to Peru.

'All back,' said Paddy to the accompaniment of a gentle whistle blast, which this time *was* angels' music in Fenner's Peruvian ears.

'But,' said Fenner as an afterthought, 'we'll have to keep her hidden between shows. Can you manage that?' he said to the girls. Could they? they each thought. After all they had hidden from Fenner over these years, to hide Jasmin would be as easy as it had been to hide Kathy's sister's wedding dress they had made in the workroom some time ago, that they had given as a wedding gift.

'Yes, Mr Fenner,' said Paddy voicing the girls' thoughts. 'We can hide her OK, now, can we get on with our bonuses?'

'Yes, dear. Of course,' said Fenner as the whirr of the sewing machines brought money to his ears. 'Let's get on with the production, girls.' He realized his headache had gone.

The bus conductor looked at the ruby sparkling in his hand as his bus pulled into its garage at the end of his shift. He didn't know if it had been stolen or smuggled into the country from any one of the many yachts that arrived in Hamble's yacht harbour from all over the world. He didn't even know if it was genuine or not. It looked real enough, but he couldn't tell. Taking pity on the Arab girl at the time seemed reasonable, but now, after he'd thought about it he wasn't sure.

'I don't know if its genuine,' said the police sergeant at the Central Police Station in Southampton, as he took the ruby from the conductor. The sergeant asked him questions about the girl and he had answered that all he knew was that this Arab girl had got on his bus at Hamble and asked how she could get to the exhibition in Southampton. The police sergeant took down the necessary particulars, his name and address and that was all he and anybody else, could do at the moment.

Basil Thornton's face dropped, as he listened to his superior in the Foreign Office at the other end of the phone. He felt at least six years of promotional advancement were draining away as he listened to the junior Minister relate the saga of the missing harem girl.

'No, Minister,' said Basil. He didn't know one of the sheikh's harem girls had defected and that the sheikh was very annoyed – so annoyed in fact, that he was considering severing his order for millions of pounds' worth of military equipment that he had intended to pay for in OIL. 'My fault well . . .' began Basil in humble protest. '. . . find her . . . yes, I'll find her, sir . . . I'd better . . . yes, sir . . . no, I shouldn't like to be assigned to Uganda, sir . . . yes, sir . . . the Tower is a chilling place . . . very good, sir . . . at once, sir . . . sooner, yes, sir.' Basil's ear rang with doom. Everything had been going so well and his promotion had seemed assured. 'If I ever find anybody who's had a hand in this,' he said to himself in a threatening tone as he dialled Southampton Police Station.

Jasmin's success as a model was immediate, for many dozens of shoppers crowded round Fenner's stand as she paraded the gowns. Paddy had found suitable music for the record player and the whole atmosphere was made electric by the very sexy movements of Jasmin, who was not new to showing off her charms in a subtle manner, for she had been taught for many years the art of seduction by the older harem girls in the sheikh's palace in her home country. The men among the shoppers, taunted by the attractions of Jasmin, eagerly agreed to spend the money on such gowns, in which they hoped their wives would find it in their innermost desires to taunt them in the same way Jasmin had. Women shoppers also gazed upon the seductiveness of Jasmin and imagined themselves moving provocatively about the house, or doing the washing-up, and seeing their husbands' heads spin round away from the football as this dream of enchantment drifted past before their very eyes, smelling of fresh desert orchids and exotic blooms and they swept all before them . . . with a vacuum cleaner.

Tony also was excelling himself at the microphone as he 'threw' in snippets of Eastern promise in his introductions and explanations of the gowns. Fenner was feeling very pleased with everything, sales were booming, and if they kept up as they were at the moment, he would have covered his expenses, especially those of the girls he had found mounting at every turn. The drinks' bill at the nightclub for instance, still left an awful pain in his pocket. But he was back with a chance to even the score and still come out all right, if things held as they were now. He reasoned, that if he had lost the Arab's order, he may well just cover himself if the sales continued to boom like this till the end of the exhibition. It would be a race against time but the prestige he must be building up for Fenner Fashions International would surely make him one of the leading gown and dress manufacturers in Europe, if not the world. It would be from his reputation that he would become rich and famous, and live in luxury having made his mark and his name a household word that people would remember for all time like Rolls-Royce, Harrods, Blooms.

'You've done marvellous,' said Paddy, congratulating Jasmin at the end of another successful show.

'Thank you,' said Jasmin as Paddy helped her out of the gown she had just modelled. 'You are very kind to me, how can I repay you?'

'That's what a union does, it brings people closer together,' said Paddy, hanging up the gown.

'Like you and Mr Fenner?'

'Well, yes,' faltered Paddy. 'Er ... we do have to get together quite a bit.'

'For sex?' asked Jasmin.

Paddy managed to stop herself from swallowing the pins she was holding in her mouth. 'Oh, no,' she coughed. 'To organize the smooth running of the factory, things like that.'

'Oh, I see,' said Jasmin, not sure.

'I mean we have to guard our rights.'

'Oh,' said Jasmin, 'like Abdul guards ours.'

'Yes, that sort of thing,' replied Paddy, thinking hard what to say.

Paddy helped dress Jasmin into ordinary workroom clothes and curled her beautiful long hair up into a bun, in an effort to make her look as unobtrusive as possible and avoid detection. Jasmin looked still very beautiful and would have done in anything she wore, but it was the only thing the girls could do to help her after she had made such a dangerous sacrifice in running away from the sheikh. They joined the girls in the workroom and Jasmin sat at a spare workroom machine, and tried to look ordinary.

'Like a cup of tea, Jas?' said Olive with open familiarity as she handed her a large mug of steaming sweet English tea.

'Haven't you got a saucer for her?' asked Paddy.

'Why? She don't drink out of the saucer, does she?'

'No,' chipped in Kathy. 'But she's our guest, ain't she?'

'How would you like a great big steaming mug like that if you were a guest in someone's house?' asked Jo-Jo.

'Well, that's what we have if we go to Arthur's mother for tea.'

'Yes, but your family then,' said Kathy, taking her own steaming mug of tea, as they had stopped for the official factory tea break.

'I don't like a great big mug like this,' said Mabel, testing her tea.

'Look,' said Paddy. 'You know Fenner, if we had little cups he'd cut down on our tea break.'

Basil Thornton's disguise was pathetic, he looked like a second-hand spy in a fourth-rate film in a ninth-rate cinema. He'd decided to spy on Fenner Fashions after a clue he'd received from the Police in conjunction with the Home and Foreign Offices. He was the only one on the side of the Law who had seen Jasmin and could identify her. The Police didn't want to arouse suspicion by the presence of their conspicuous uniform. The sheikh or Abdul would have been recognized by Jasmin and the Foreign Minister certainly wasn't going to 'clear up' after Basil. So Basil it had to be. His disguise had consisted of a long, dirty, off-white raincoat – the type 'flashers' used in the parks – over a dark suit, his official FO suit. An old black Homberg hat bought from the same shop as the coat, and a most ludicrous long black beard that he might have got from the corpse of Rasputin.

'No tramps allowed in here,' said the exhibition doorman immediately upon Basil's arrival.

'I'm from the Foreign Office,' said Basil out of the side of his mouth.

'Very foreign by the look of you,' said the doorman not budging from Basil's path.

Basil fumbled in his raincoat pocket and pulled out a dirty plastic bag, into which he'd placed his official papers in case he had to take to the water to escape capture. He'd seen this ruse in a James Bond film and it had been a worthwhile safeguard.

'Don't bribe me with sandwiches,' said the doorman backing away. 'I suppose you get them out of a dustbin.'

Basil fumbled in the bag and found his official identification papers and 'flashed' them to the doorman. This did not have the response Basil had expected. That of the doorman grovelling at his feet for forgiveness.

'Either you've found these or they're genuine,' said the diligent doorman. 'I'll let you in this time, but any trouble from you and you'll be out on your ear.'

Basil sheepishly passed into the exhibition hall and mingled with the crowd who avoided him as though he was the plague in person, so mingling for Basil became difficult. Realizing he had overdone his disguise he looked round for a Gents in which he could modify it slightly.

Upon entering a nearby loo, the attendant immediately advised him in no uncertain terms. 'Don't you flash in my toilet, mate, or I'll wallop you with this bucket.'

Basil gained the sanctuary of a vacant WC and locked himself in for safety. With a cigarette lighter, all he had to use, he singed off the beard he had stuck on his face to a more realistic size, and folded the raincoat over his arm and set his Homberg hat at a more rakish angle, then undoing the lock on the door he stepped out, a 'new' man, and went over to the mirror to check his very much improved disguise. Standing next to him was an older man washing his hands, having come out of the cubicle next to the one Basil had occupied for his 'quick change act'. The man sniffed loudly at the smell of burning beard and said to Basil, ' 'Ere mate. You been on the pot?'

Basil made his way through the crowded exhibition hall attracting less attention in his improved disguise. To Basil this was a 'mission of mercy', hoping that his superior would have mercy on his career and promotion, if he could discover the missing Jasmin. Also this would abate the sheikh's anger at losing her, which in turn, he hoped, would restore relations between him and Great Britain. He shuddered to think that this whole saga had come to *him*, who stood on the threshold of his Foreign Office ambitions, after waiting so long in very junior office. He just *had* to find Jasmin and restore her to her rightful owner, to save his own personal lifetime dreams of rising power. He moved with caution along the aisles of the hall, dodging from one crowded stand to the next as he made his way to his goal. As he neared Fenner's stand he could see it was empty, both on the stand and in front where the shoppers usually stood watching the fashion show. He had time to kill, for he knew that the fashion shows were held hourly from when he had brought the sheikh to the exhibition before. His task was to discover whether or not Jasmin had defected to Fenner Fashions and report to his superior at the Foreign Office as to his findings. From all the reports that had been passed to him from various sources, he had a pretty good idea she was here, knowing that her only contact outside the harem had been with Fenner Fashions on the sheikh's yacht. But it was vital to establish the definite proof.

Basil hovered around the stands nearest to Fenner's, in order to keep his eye open for any movement which might lead to clues, and to keep himself hidden at the same time.

'Good morning, Rabbi,' said an eager salesman at Basil's elbow, as he stood near a stand opposite Fenner's. Basil didn't take any notice, not being a Rabbi himself, but stood unobtrusively reading a pamphlet, one eye glued on Fenner's stand. 'Shalom and good morning,' said the persistent salesman, trying to add a little friendly language and this time tugging Basil's sleeve. Basil turned to the grinning salesman and nodded.

'Do you speak English?' asked the salesman.

Basil nearly blurted out that of course he spoke English, Oxford English, in fact they all spoke it at my school, wouldn't have got in otherwise. He restrained his impulses as he looked at the salesman, who perhaps wouldn't be interested in his degree in Anglo-Saxon languages. But then again, being a keen type, he may well have and Basil was a bit rusty on his schoolday learnings, so he kept a still tongue and considered how effective his disguise must be.

'A leetle,' he said.

'Well, sir,' continued the salesman. 'Our wall cavity insulation is the best in Britain and of course, sir,' he paused in readiness to deliver the final blow, 'we export to Israel.' The salesman went on endlessly with his rehearsed sales talk, handing Basil a pamphlet to substantiate its authenticity. 'Reduces heating bills by thirty per cent,' he continued, handing Basil yet another pamphlet. Soon Basil had an armful of pamphlets and enough details to add another degree with honours in Thermal Insulation, to his Anglo-Saxon languages. 'I mean,' said the salesman, 'those winds are draughty coming off the Golan Heights and you'll need to be kept warm.' He was only trying to bring in a little local background colour for the Rabbi. Basil, still with his eye on Fenner's stand, listened half-heartedly to the salesman's sell as it bored its way into his mind. Doesn't this fool realize, thought Basil, that if I were a Rabbi visitor and might well have have come from Israel, the last thing I would have wanted in that sun-drenched land was heat from a HOT HOUSE! Basil allowed the deception to continue, wondering if this nit also sold freezer units to Eskimos?

'Yes, sir. We can guarantee to keep your igloo at freezing point indefinitely.' Basil imagined the salesman saying. 'We have a saying in our trade,' he would lie. 'Our thermal mesh keeps the blubber fresh.' I suppose, thought Basil, he would also flog 'our large model to keep whales in deep freeze'. He could just imagine the Eskimo wife gutting and preparing a whale for her husband's tea and casually tossing the head to the cat. Saved by the bell 'music', thought Basil as he listened with joy to a rather scratched rendering of the Luton Girls' Choir singing 'The Sheikh of Araby' coming from Fenner's stand, announcing their forthcoming fashion show. Basil handed back the two armfuls of literature the salesman had given him.

'We can insulate any wall, sir,' said the salesman. 'What sort of house do you live in?'

'A tent,' said Basil, as he moved to join the gathering crowd at Fenner's stand, leaving the exhausted salesman perspiring in his own insulation of shiny paper pamphlets.

Tony began his compèring by introducing Fenner, 'the man behind it all' to the gathered throng. In more ways than one, thought Basil hiding at the back of the thick crowd. He listened as Tony went on about Fenner Fashions and their creative ability, and the alteration service they offered on the spot. 'And now,' he announced, 'here is our first creation.'

Basil cowered in the crowd behind a large lady and peeked at the figure stepping on to the stand's stage. To bring a tinge of difference to the show, Jo-Jo had offered to model a dress, as she put it, 'To add a touch of colour.' Basil stared at Jo-Jo's ample but short form, looking quite desirable in the gown she wore, then his gaze moved up to her face, her even shining teeth shone against their black background and hastily confirmed in Basil's mind that this girl was not Jasmin. His heart sank three places as the thought and possibility of Jasmin not being there at all seemed appropriate. The large lady in front of Basil moved forward to the stand, captivated by the gown Jo-Jo wore and seeing herself looking as desirable. This move had to some degree blown Basil's cover, and quickly he stooped around in the crowd looking for another hiding place. The wide shoulders and bell-bottomed trousers of two sailors in the crowd hid the disguised Basil admirably. Basil even thanked the Admiral for allowing them leave.

'Coo, I couldn't half give her one,' said one uncouth sailor as Kathy took the stage before them.

'She'd be heaven in the hammock,' added the other uncouth youth.

Basil's heaven of promotion sank even further as he gazed unhappily at Kathy, knowing she definitely wasn't Jasmin. A Foreign Office job in Uganda loomed nearer in his mind. Basil imagined, as he stood in the sweltering crowd, being shown to his mud hut accommodation on a FO hill station in the middle of Uganda, complete, he could almost imagine, with cavity wall insulation to keep him warm. He began to faint at the stifling heat of the crowd that had insulated him by their number. An instant wave of cool refreshing air seemed to revive him completely as Jasmin's beauty stepped upon the stage. 'That's the one I've been looking for,' he gasped quietly but aloud.

'You dirty old Rabbi,' said one uncouth sailor turning to smile at Basil's exclamation.

'What, have you run out of nuns?' asked the other.

Gleefully, having made a definite identification of Jasmin, Basil headed for the nearest telephone to relate the urgent news to his superior, before he issued Basil's travel tickets for Uganda.

The ocelot fur coat fitted Mrs Fenner beautifully as she stepped from the taxi, but didn't somehow look as good as the genuine beaver lamb coat her mother wore as she followed her out of the cab. 'One fifty?' queried Mrs Fenner as she paid the cabbie. 'I didn't think Southampton taxis were as expensive as London.' The Polygon Hotel porters collected the luggage from the taxi and followed Mrs Fenner and her mother to reception. They stood nearby waiting for the ladies to register.

'Fenner of Fenner Fashions International,' said Mrs Fenner. 'Mrs Fenner.'

The porters' faces dropped as they heard that name. For far back in the annals of tipping, their minds recalled a certain meanness associated with that name. 'You take it on your own 'arry,' said a considerate mate as they stood near the Fenner baggage. 'It won't be worth it for two of us.'

The porter collected the luggage. A lot for one night, he thought, and accompanied the ladies to their room via the lift and corridors.

'Thank you, put them down there,' said Mrs Fenner, indicating a place to 'arry.

'Thank you,' said Harry as he crumpled a new pound note into his porter's waistcoat pocket, as his faith was renewed in at least one member of the Fenner clan.

'A pound!' said Mrs Fenner's mother, remembering her poor childhood.

'Fenner Fashions International is a household name now, mother dear,' she said, oblivious to the fact that it was also well known in parts of Arabia and England's Foreign Office. 'We mustn't appear mean in front of the staff here.' She crossed to the room service telephone on the bedside table. 'Mrs Fenner here. Room five o four. Send up coffee for two and a few cream cakes, and what time is dinner? . . . Thank you,' she said, replacing the receiver.

On the assumed success of Fenner's trade at the exhibition, Mrs Fenner and her mother had decided to pay a flying visit to Southampton, after their shopping spree in London.

'The air would do us good,' suggested Mrs Fenner, so they had 'upped and gone'. Besides, she wanted the chance to show off her new fur coat in a city other than London, but most of all she wanted to share in the fame and bright lights of her husband Harold's success at becoming international. Though the most deep and dark intention in her and her mother's mind was to see what Harold was up to, with his love for spending other people's money on other people's 'birds'. She, Mrs Fenner, had been a model herself, and knew all the things that went on in the rag trade with the girls in the workroom and *those* models, looking for a quick rich husband, as they pranced around half-naked getting ready to model the next creation. I'm up to all their tricks, she thought, overlooking the fact that she'd done the same.

'So we meet again Mr Fenner,' said Mr Bootle, sounding like D'Artagnan of *The Three Musketeers* at last face to face with his mortal enemy. Fenner, standing in Bootle's temporary office in the exhibition hall looked bewildered and wondered what could be wrong now.

'I've got the Foreign Office on the phone . . . for you.' It was like a rapier thrust.

'Oh, I wonder what they want?' said Fenner sheepishly, getting a sickly feeling in his sinking stomach.

'I just can't bring myself to tell you,' said Bootle with the ring of the whole story of Jasmin's defection right here in his very own exhibition, still ringing in his ears.

Fenner picked up the telephone receiver which lay on Bootle's desk and shakily put it to his ear. 'Harold Fenner,' he piped in a high shrill voice of fear and trepidation. Bootle enjoyed watching Fenner's face drain from its bone structure, knowing what the Foreign Office Minister was saying.

'. . . harbouring a fugitive?' repeated Fenner into the phone with surprise '. . . me . . . England's survival . . . what oil? . . . guilty of treason?' The barrage of assaults against Fenner Fashions and the repercussions they had caused, silenced Fenner from any protesting statements, he just listened to his empire crumbling before his very ears. My girls, he thought as he listened, they've gone too far this time, with their bloody women's lib and sex equality. He sank slowly on to the hard chair in Bootle's office and didn't feel a thing from its hard seat on his. I could be shot for this, he thought, seriously shot. He replaced the red hot phone in its cradle and sniffed a whisp of burning ear then, rising to his feet, began to walk out of Bootle's office. He thought he heard Bootle's horns being sharpened as Bootle screamed and demanded Fenner Fashions to leave the exhibition at once, and never to darken Southampton's doorstep again. He walked in a daze past a giggling secretary and out into the exhibition hall, he felt the eyes of the world were upon him. He visualized thousands of people blaming him for the downfall of England. The refugee columns would already be on the move from places he'd never heard of like, Warsash, Bursledon, Botley, all pushing prams with a few hurriedly collected personal items and family treasures piled in them. The rich were bribing people who owned large removal vans with gold and silver in order to make good their escape from the sinking nation. Mothers were thrusting their babies at him screaming, 'Remember this man all your life. *He* brought down England, and he's the cause your father's at the front now.'

Fenner's walk revived his blood that had ceased pumping through his body. 'Those girls,' he whispered aloud, as he loaded his tongue with deadly nerve gas.

Fenner walked defiantly to his stand, crossed the stage, burst through the curtains at the back and into the workroom where the girls hurriedly resumed work at his arrival. Looking straight ahead, he made his way directly to Paddy as the girls watched in silence, reached for the whistle that hung round her neck, put it to his lips, and blew such a blast that it sent seagulls again screeching into the air on the Isle of Wight; a Portsmouth striker kicked a penalty before the ref had blown *his* whistle; and an old lady turned down her hearing aid in nearby Chichester. The girls held their ears and stared at Fenner in amazement, only Paddy's courage spoke.

'That's Union property Mr Fenner.'

Fenner seethed to a high level. 'Union property, by the time I've finished with your Union the only property you'll own is the skin on your bodies.'

Even Paddy was taken back at Fenner's obvious madness to say such a thing and for once in her life was speechless.

'Do you know?' continued Fenner in fiendish tone, 'I have just been accused of treason by the Foreign Minister of all England. I've been held responsible for this country's financial failure, the deficit of our balance of payments has been laid squarely at the door of Fenner Fashions.' Not having the heart to add International. 'And all because of *you.*' He pointed at Paddy. 'You have taught this Jezabel Jasmin sex equality with your Union talk and the sheikh has cancelled his oil supply to

Great Britain forever, because his favourite harem girl has defected not to Finland or France, but to Fenner Fashions.' He collapsed into a vacant workroom chair.

The girls sat silent for a while until Olive asked, 'Would you like a cup of tea, Mr Fenner?'

'It did marvels for people who were bombed out during the war,' added Mabel in sympathy.

'I'll help you,' said Jo-Jo to Olive as she moved to help get the tea, but still keeping her eye on Fenner who was toying with a large pair of pinking shears on the workroom table.

'Now, let's get this straight,' said Paddy, composing herself. 'Because that dirty old sheikh has lost one of his hundred harem girls, he's done all this?'

'Not just one,' said Fenner more calmly. '*The* one, his bloody favourite, of all of them to choose from, you and only you would have to pick on her.'

'Well what's that got to do with you if she chooses to 'op it from the 'arem?'

'They think I did it, and that I'm harbouring a fugitive.'

'Rubbish,' said Paddy back to her old self. 'She came here on her own.'

'She wouldn't have thought about it if you hadn't put her in the picture. Now we'll lose the sheikh's order. I've been ordered off these premises immediately and by the time my firm and *your* union, don't forget, have paid compensation to the Exchequer for loss of earnings for England I shall be so overdrawn at the bank they'll think they bank with me.'

'Well the answer's simple,' said Paddy in a moment of genius. 'We'll kidnap Jasmin and hold her for ransom.'

Fenner felt all his old complaints coming on at Paddy's suggestion, and also the chill of what Abdul's sword would do to his neck. 'You must be joking,' he whimpered.

'No,' said Paddy. 'He's put the squeeze on the government, who in turn's put the squeeze on you, and all because of Jasmin – so we'll reverse the squeeze. We hold the trump card, don't we, dear?' she asked Jasmin who had been sitting with the girls in her 'worker's' disguise.

'Yes,' she said sweetly but without understanding a word of what had been said or its complications.

'Leave it to us, Mr Fenner,' said Paddy. 'I've got a plan to get us all out of this.'

'Well, I suppose death by a firing squad is as quick as Abdul's sword.' Fenner was totally dismayed by it all, and not really caring if he lived or died at this moment of time. Olive arrived with the tea, and Jo-Jo followed her, peering to see who Fenner had 'pinked' with the scissors. Fenner and Tony, the girls and Jasmin all took hot mugs of steaming comforting tea and waited for Paddy to dig them all out of the rubble with her plan.

Paddy began, 'Look, they've traced Jasmin to us here, and they're probably on their way to collect her; now then, *if* she isn't here when they arrive there's not much they can do about it; if we tart up Jasmin to look like someone else and hide her away somewhere – we'll quietly ask the sheikh if he wants her back, call off the dogs.'

Fenner was past thinking about what would happen to them if they were found out, and asked, 'Where do we hide Jasmin – she might have to stay a couple of days?'

'Where there's a lot of people *and* where she can stay,' said Paddy.

'How about that nice hotel we went to when we first came?' said Lynn.

'The Polygon?'

'Brilliant. She'd be lost in the crowds that stay there and if she didn't look like a harem girl, who'd know?'

'Would she stay there on her own?' asked Kathy.

'No, we'll have to think about that a bit.'

' 'Ere,' said Jo-Jo. 'What about if Jasmin was an old lady and stayed in the hotel with Mabel? They'll be looking for a young girl, not an old maid.'

'Thank you,' said Mabel at the comparison.

'It's for the good of us all,' said Olive. 'I don't want to end up in the Tower, what would Arthur say?'

They ignored what Arthur would have thought for the moment; there were more important considerations.

'See?' said Paddy confidently. 'It wouldn't be like really kidnapping, because it's what Jasmin wants, so she'll be a willing party, and all we've done is help a poor girl in distress.'

'Dis dress or dat dress?' laughed Jo-Jo.

'Let's get on with it, OK?' said Paddy. 'Mr Fenner, you book a twin-bedded room at the Polygon for Jasmin and Mabel.'

'And Twinky,' added Mabel.

'And Twinky,' continued Paddy. 'And we'll make Jasmin look like an old lady. Tony, lay on a cab to take them when we're ready. Don't worry Mr Fenner, we'll do it all.'

'That's what worries me,' said Fenner, holding his head in despair.

Paddy's plan swept into action as each of them set out to complete their alloted tasks. Jasmin's clothes were quickly made in the workroom at a breathtaking speed that Fenner would have applauded. Odd make-up from the girls' handbags was collected to help the transformation of the beautiful Jasmin's face, and a head scarf hid her black tresses. A sober pair of Mabel's shoes thankfully fitted Jasmin's feet, and instructions to use a slight crouch as she walked completed the ensemble. Jasmin, the beautiful harem girl, was now a diminutive old lady with a slight crouch, and in the company of Mabel and Twinky was 'smuggled' out through the back curtains of the workroom to the waiting cab Tony had booked. Everything had gone off like a well-oiled operation of which the Foreign Office would be justly proud.

'That's fine,' said Fenner into a telephone near the exhibition hall. 'One twin-bedded room with bathroom for my two elderly aunties ... what number room? Five o six. OK. Thank you again,' he said, ringing off.

Sheikh Ali Achmud, accompanied by Abdul and Basil Thornton, stormed into his yellow Rolls-Royce and demanded of the chauffeur, 'Your head, if you're not there in ten minutes.' The chauffeur, having over the years grown accustomed to his head, set Hamble Lane alight with searing rubber as he pushed the Rolls to its limits. He reasoned the sheikh would always pay the fines for speeding and dangerous driving, but no money in the world could replace his severed head.

'Shouldn't we say a short prayer or something?' said Fenner having rejoined the girls in the workroom.

'We've got to be calm,' said Paddy. 'A lot depends on how we handle it.'

'Drink this,' said Kathy handing Fenner another mug of tea. Being much cooler than their previous brews, he took a long, long draught to moisten his parched throat. The steam from Fenner's mouth would have convinced anyone watching that the tea was in fact hot, but those who knew better would have seen Kathy empty a half bottle of whisky in the tea pot before she served it to everybody. The Dutch courage worked well in the face of Arabian wrath and Foreign Office hysterics from Basil, as the sheikh lashed everyone in sight with his tongue in the tiny workroom at the back of Fenner's stand. After all and sundry had had curses laid upon their heads from the sheikh, ranging from 'death by a thousand cuts' to the proverbial 'boiled in oil', the sheikh took a short breather to invent some even more gruesome penalties for the entire Fenner Fashion strain.

During this short lull, Paddy, on everybody's behalf, and strengthened by the whisky announced, 'Now hold on a minute, sheikh.' All eyes were turned towards Paddy, attracted by the defiant tone in her voice which Fenner knew so well. 'Your favourite girlfriend came to us in trouble and we helped her out.'

The sheikh looked astounded at Fenner, saying, 'Do you allow your woman to speak in such a manner?'

Fenner, smiling gently on a cloud of highland brew, said, 'Well, things over here are different, your sheikhness.'

'This mere woman speaks for you all?'

Fenner and the girls nodded in confirmation. 'Frequently,' said Fenner, smiling at Paddy and inviting her to continue.

'Well,' Paddy went on. 'Jasmin arrived here, tired and hungry, with no money, and nowhere to go; we could have turned her out on the streets in a strange city, in a strange land, but we didn't,' said Paddy, gaining everyone's attention as she spoke. 'We gave her food and clothes and cared for her and at her insistence she repaid us by doing a bit of modelling.'

'That surely is the calibre of Jasmin,' said the sheikh remorsefully.

'Don't forget, sheikh,' continued Paddy, 'this is a sea-port, and no telling what might have happened to her if we'd let her go; she might have been carted off to some foreign broth . . . house, and we'd never have seen her again.'

The sheikh sank on to a workroom chair and held his head in his hands. 'Where is she now?' he began to sob.

'Oh, don't cry,' said Kathy, comfortingly.

'No, that won't help,' said Jo-Jo brightly.

'Of all the loves of my life,' wept the sheikh, 'the lovely

Jasmin is the fairest of them all. She above all has comforted me in my times of greatest stress and it's for her I have given my undying love till all the oases run dry and the palm trees wilt to dust; my dearest Jasmin . . .'

Olive and Lynn were crying their eyes out unable to speak, whilst Basil tried hard to swallow the lump in his throat; gone were the thoughts of promotion. Paddy sniffed herself to her senses and deemed the moment for their deliverance at hand. 'If we can get her back,' began Paddy.

'Anything in this world shall be yours,' the sheikh interrupted.

'Hers?' jumped in Fenner, suddenly sober.

'Ours,' corrected Paddy sharply.

'Will you restore friendly relations with England then?' demanded Paddy majestically.

'Immediately,' said the sheikh with a wave of permission to Basil. 'Now bring her to me.'

'What about your dress order?' piped in Fenner taking the opportunity for business.

'Granted,'

'Very well. Mr Fenner will go to the secret hiding place and bring Jasmin here,' said Paddy, hoping to get rid of Fenner before he cocked everything up.

'I must make a phone call,' said Basil, leaving urgently.

'I shall make you a nice cup of tea,' sniffled Olive to the sheikh, 'as though you were my very own . . . Arthur,' she corrected herself hurriedly.

'Lynn, you phone Mabel and give her the news. Mr Fenner, these are the clothes for Jasmin we've made, you know, instead of her disguise,' winked Paddy to Fenner who looked like a fish out of water at all the speedy happenings.

'With all speed Mr Fenner,' urged the sheikh, 'and may the spirit of the desert go with you. And you young lady,' he turned to Paddy. 'How would you like to be my manageress?'

'Why, have you got a dress factory out where you live?'

'No sweet child,' said the sheikh. 'I mean of my harem.'

Paddy looked straight at Abdul standing silent and very large. 'No thanks,' she decided. 'I can handle Mr Fenner, but I don't know about him.' She nodded towards Abdul.

At the hotel, Fenner had sent Mabel to hold a taxi for the

return journey to the exhibition, whilst he waited in the bedroom for Jasmin to change into her 'new' clothes the girls had made for her, in the bathroom. Putting the 'old lady's' clothes in the suitcase he'd brought, Fenner accompanied Jasmin, again looking beautiful in her new outfit from Fenner Fashions, to the door of the room. As he stepped into the corridor with Jasmin a scream greeted his ears. It was a scream he knew well and his heart that had taken such a beating over the last few days began to palpitate again furiously, as he turned to see his wife and mother-in-law coming out of their bedroom opposite. Fenner's heart, stomach and liver were in his mouth.

'Just as I thought,' shrieked Mrs Fenner to her mother. 'The minute my back is turned he's up to his old tricks.'

'You should be ashamed, Harold,' said his mother-in-law, as Fenner cowered behind Jasmin.

'I knew it, I knew it,' repeated his wife hysterically. 'He's got this model girl showing clothes all day, and then showing herself to him at night; oh the shame of it all.'

'Now, dear,' began Fenner still sheltering behind Jasmin. 'I can explain . . . you see *this* girl, Jasmin, is the favourite harem girl of this oil sheikh.'

Fenner's mother-in-law held her hands over her ears. 'Harold, please. It's bad enough we should catch you out. Please don't lie.'

'Oil sheikh.' said his wife from the bottom of her throat. 'And I suppose he's ordered ten thousand pounds' worth of dresses for the harem from you.'

'Exactly,' said Fenner with conviction, peering over Jasmin's shoulder.

'And I suppose he's over here buying supplies for Arabia?' said his mother-in-law.

'Yes, right again.' Fenner could see all his past lives appearing before him.

'Are these two ladies in your harem like the girls at your factory?' asked Jasmin inquisitively.

'Oh spirit of the desert, I thought you were ordered to come with me,' said Fenner, appealing to the heavens with his hands as Jasmin dropped her bomb.

'Others in his harem, eh?' said Fenner's wife.

'It gets worse,' said her mother, 'and to think he used to be such a nice boy.'

'Yes,' said Mrs Fenner scathingly. 'The nice boy's now a dirty old man.'

'Look, look,' said Fenner praying for deliverance, as several other residents looked out of their bedroom doors at the commotion. 'I've got to go to the exhibition to return Jasmin.' Everybody heard him above the din.

'God!' said his mother-in-law. 'She's on hire?'

'Come to the exhibition with me and you'll see,' suggested Fenner confidently, sensing a crack in the tension.

'You're right, I'm coming to that den of iniquity. Come along mother, *I* need a witness.'

In the taxi to the exhibition the only one who spoke was Twinky, but no one would listen; they all sat in silence and glared at each other. Twinky did his wee in the taxi and barked as if to say, 'I did ask.'

Back in the workroom at the exhibition, the sight of a real live oil sheikh shook Mrs Fenner to the roots of her mock ocelot, as it did her mother, whose genuine beaver lamb bleated. The sight of Jasmin to the sheikh made the oil run faster in his veins as he caressed her, thanking Allah in person for his deliverance from a lonely life. As for the girls, there wasn't a 'dry' bonus in the house, as each of them grabbed a piece of Paddy and chaired her round the workroom in honour of her leadership in her firm's hour of need. Fenner was almost as tall as Abdul with vindication from the lifetime anger of his personal women he might well have suffered. Basil who had finished making and taking his multi-telephone calls to and from his superior, gleamed as brightly as any newly promoted Foreign Office devotee would. Uganda was a far-flung corner of the earth, that would not feel the tread of Basil Thornton's feet. Whilst the jubilations were at their height, Basil whispered into Fenner's ear, 'Can I have a quiet word with you Mr Fenner?'

'Certainly, my boy,' said Fenner, as the two men moved to a quieter part of the workroom.

'I've had a word with my superior at the Foreign Office and they've arranged a feast at the Polygon Hotel in honour of the sheikh, as a gesture of good will, you know?'

'What a splendid idea,' said Fenner, also revelling in the restored relations with the sheikh's money.

'Apparently, the highest mark of respect one can afford a

sheikh is to hold a Mutton Grab in his honour, so our chappies at the Foreign Office have arranged it all.'

'Well, it sounds a wonderful idea.'

'Everybody is of course invited.'

'My girls?'

'Certainly, if you wish.'

'And Tony?'

'Why not? There will be enough for everyone. Of course Arabs do not drink, but I'm sure the sheikh wouldn't object to dinner wine, if you see what I mean?'

'First class idea,' said Fenner. 'After all, we've all gained from restoring relations haven't we?'

'Quite so, quite so. Then shall we say nine o'clock at the Polygon then?'

'Nine o'clock on the dot.' And the two men shook hands.

Fenner entered Bootle's office for yet a third time, but this time it had been by an invitation letter typed by the elder typist and delivered by the younger typist by hand.

'Oh, do come in, Mr Fenner,' said Bootle, rising to greet him. Fenner entered the office shown in by the younger typist who didn't seem to dare to giggle. 'Please, may I offer you a seat,' said Bootle, offering Fenner his usual hard seat.

'Oh, thank you.' Fenner took Bootle's own desk chair, padded and comfortable. Fenner had guessed correctly by the changed attitude of Bootle and his staff, that Basil had used this office to telephone, to convey the good news to his superiors at the Foreign Office, and that he had related that same news to Bootle.

'Glass of sherry?' said Bootle as the younger typist entered with a tray upon which stood two glasses of sherry and the bottle. Fenner enjoyed the attention he was receiving from Bootle; he enjoyed being important. It gave him a feeling of power, and as Fenner Fashions supplied Bootle's with dresses, it was going to cement their trading partnership even more firmly.

'Thank you,' said Fenner taking the sherry and sipping it. 'Mmm, it's a very good one,' not really knowing the difference from any other.

'Good,' said Bootle eager to please, and he sat on the hard chair adjusting his posterior to fit. 'Well, I'd just like to say that after a lot of misunderstandings, on our part I hasten to say,' he added as Fenner gave him an inquiring look. 'But of course the worry of the exhibition . . . you know how it is?'

Fenner didn't know how it was, but he just sat and enjoyed Bootle, who was not below Fenner's degree.

'Well, in short,' went on Bootle. 'I just wanted to say that as the exhibition has been so successful, we have decided to have another one next year, and of course we should like to have the name of Fenner Fashions . . .'

'International,' added Fenner.

'Er . . . quite,' said Bootle hastily. 'Fenner Fashions International.'

Fenner nodded and smiled as Bootle went on. 'International, proudly along with our own.'

'Yes,' said Fenner revelling in these moments. 'I think that can be arranged. I'll get my deputy to fix up something here of course. I shall be supervising our European branches in Paris and Arabia.'

'Of course,' said Bootle, wondering which part of Europe, Arabia came into. 'Yes.' He shifted in his hard seat. 'I was . . . er, wondering,' he hesitated, 'as you obviously know the sheikh very well . . .'

'Oh, intimately,' boasted Fenner. 'I mean you can't get much closer to a man than dressing his bits of crum . . . er, fancy pieces, so to speak, can one?'

'Quite,' Bootle agreed, filling Fenner's drained sherry glass. 'Well, er, perhaps you, would consider . . . er, exporting some of our wares along with your own?'

'Why not?' said Fenner draining his sherry in one tight-lipped suck. 'We'll have branches everywhere of course, and even where we've not, we'll be known!'

'Oh, that's wonderful,' said Bootle rising to end the meeting before Fenner drained the sherry bottle.

'Just the usual commission,' said Fenner. 'Handling charge you know.'

'Quite.' Bootle always said 'quite'.

'Oh, I suppose fifteen per cent, something like that,' said Fenner whilst the going was going good.

'Fifteen?' queried Bootle, reaching for his own sherry.

'Yes. Perhaps that's a bit low.' Fenner leaned back in Bootle's chair.

'Oh no, fifteen's fine,' said Bootle quickly, crossing to open the office door. 'Well I'm sure you've got lots to do . . .'

Fenner rose and strode proudly out of the office. 'Pity your girls don't smile a bit more,' he said a little sarcastically as he left.

CHAPTER EIGHT

In the specially decorated banqueting-room at the Polygon, everybody who had been invited to the 'Mutton Grab' sat on cushions round a huge roasted sheep on an even huger silver platter, all dressed in their finery for the occasion. It lay there on a bed of rice and was complete except for its fleecy skin. However, its head was as normal and it lay there, looking very unhappy by the look in its sad eyes, but it still proudly displayed a large pair of spiralled horns. The sheikh sat at the head of the dish facing the sheep's soulful eyes – the exalted position, while Fenner wondered if his place facing the sheep's rear was also exalted. Jasmin, Sahleet and Camilla flanked the sheikh's right hand, and Mrs Fenner and her mother gave a tingling giggle when the sheikh announced to the two ladies, but addressing Mrs Fenner, 'You shall sit on my left hand.'

'I wouldn't do that, ducks,' whispered Kathy to Olive. 'He's got a very fast left.' And they joined the other girls who were seated either side of the sheep, as were Basil and Tony. Abdul, towered behind the sheikh to oversee his safety.

Finger bowls containing warm water and pieces of lemon were placed at every setting, alone with large white table napkins. The sheikh made a short speech on the pleasure of accepting the 'Mutton Grab' in his honour, and explained briefly that all the diners needed to do was in fact 'grab' the piece of mutton of their fancy, tear it off the carcass, and eat it. Each of the diners stared at the section of sheep in front of them, then looked at the Arab for guidance. He drew his waist dagger and poked out a sheep's eye. 'Mr Fenner,' he called to Fenner, who, seeing this, had tried to hide behind the sheep's backside. 'In grateful thanks for all you've done,' said the sheikh, smiling at Jasmin, 'I bestow upon you this great delicacy.' He leaned forward offering the sheep's eye, staring at him from the point of the dagger. Fenner fought back the natural desire to be sick, as all the girls giggled at his honoured prominence.

'You'll be able to keep an eye on us now all right,' laughed Paddy, as Fenner's expression changed to a smile.

'Well, sheikh,' Fenner began, 'though I would have been so honoured, the real person behind Jasmin's rescue was really Paddy here.'

'Yes, yes,' called Jasmin to the sheikh. 'She arranged everything.'

'So be it,' said the sheikh, turning the sheep's eye to gaze at Paddy.

The girls roared at this, as Paddy summoning all her courage, took the eye from the end of the dagger and closed her eyes in prayer.

'Fortunately, Mr Fenner, the sheep is a thoughtful creature and Allah has seen fit not to disappoint you,' said the sheikh who had meanwhile spiked the sheep's other eye on his dagger and offered it to him.

Fenner's face had drained of smile and colour. Gingerly he took the eye and prayed for this supposed spirit of the desert who seemed to have gone on strike, to come forward and picket his mouth. The calls from the girls to Paddy and Fenner contained a wide range of witticisms.

'Eye, eye,' said Kathy.

'It's about time you saw eye to eye with Paddy,' said Jo-Jo.

'Would you like my glasses?' said Olive offering them to Paddy and Fenner.

'Eye, eye, eye, Aurora,' sang Lynn, with a song from the past.

'You mutton eat it,' roared Tony.

After all the cat calls had died down Paddy looked straight into Fenner's three eyes and said, 'Mr Fenner, us leaders and all that, you know, and think of the export orders?'

To the roar of applause from the other diners, the two eyes went their separate ways as Paddy and Fenner swallowed in harmony. Both participants clutched their stomachs as the eyes within seemed to look around first for a suitable place to settle. Neither was sick. They concluded the eyes were here to stay. In jubilation, Fenner and Paddy shook hands to deafening cheers from all of the others, including the sheikh, who couldn't personally have performed the same feat as he detested sheep's eyes. The ice broken, the sheep grab began, as each of the hungry diners tore at the delicious meat and devoured it. The conversation was very enjoyable as the pleasant evening continued. It was made more pleasant by a horde of waiters who served iced champagne, as a special concession from the sheikh. The delicious best-quality champagne urged on in easy fashion the bright conversation between the 'Mutton grabbers.'

'Are you new to the firm?' Fenner's mother-in-law asked Olive who was sitting next to her.

'Oh, no,' said Olive, tearing a rib from the sheep. 'I've been under Mr Fenner for two years now.'

'Oh, thought Fenner's mother-in-law, sorry that she'd asked and eating a dainty morsel of fore-hock of sheep.

'Have you been in the Foreign Office long,' Jo-Jo asked Basil.

'Since I left college,' he replied, rinsing his fingers in the bowl.

'I expect you get to see a lot of foreign,' said Jo-Jo as Basil avoided a strange piece of meat which seemed to inform him it was male.

'Very foreign,' he said, trying another part of the sheep's anatomy and thinking how close he'd come to administrating thousands of Jo-Jo's countrymen.

'Tongue, Mrs Fenner?' said the sheikh, stretching the sheep's tongue out and placing his knife at various places along it, waiting for her to indicate how much she wanted.

'Oh, not for me. I've just had a piece of scrag end,' she said showing her upbringing.

'You're the little woman behind the great man then?' said the sheikh.

Just a little backroom girl,' she said humbly as she looked, only to see Fenner behind, then turned her gaze away quickly as she noted it was the sheep's behind.

'And very charming too, may I add?' said the sheikh just as Mrs Fenner was about to take a bit of scrag end.

'Thank you,' she answered, smiling behind a four-pound piece of meat dripping gravy, then lowered it quickly so the sheikh wouldn't think she was scrag end.

After the intimate conversations, the free flowing champagne broadened the scope across the disappearing carcass.

'You're not eating much, Mr Fenner,' said Paddy, smiling. 'Shall I reach up the front end for a piece?'

'Thank you, Paddy, I've had enough from that end, I'll make do with this.' He tore off a leg which needed two hands to lift.

Mabel, who had sat all this time in silence feeding Twinky who now looked like a very pregnant poodle from all the sheep he had devoured, said quietly to Paddy, 'Are we expected to eat a whole sheep?'

'I don't know. I suppose it's all right for the sheikh when he's at home – all his tribe digs in.'

'Well, I wondered if I could have a few bones to take home for Twinky?'

'Yes, help yourself,' said Paddy as the champagne tickled her nose. 'Would you like the horns?'

The other girls overhearing Paddy all laughed at her suggestion and Mabel sank in embarrassment at their comments.

'They'd make a good pair of handlebars for your bike,' said Kathy finishing her third glass of 'champers'.

'Or hair curlers,' giggled Lynn.

'Fancy going to bed in them,' said Olive.

'Arthur would be pleased,' giggled Jo-Jo.

'A bit more for him to hang on to,' said Paddy with a gurgling champagne giggle.

'Ooooh, you are rude,' said Olive draining her glass, only to have it filled by the attentive waiters. 'Arthur sleeps like a log anyway.'

'Well, if you wanted to wake him up,' said Kathy, 'you could butt him.'

'You always said he gets your goat,' laughed Paddy.

The evening continued with everybody in a happy frame of mind; they had all had as much as they could eat and drink and the conversations had been constant with everybody talking to each other across the sheep's now depleted carcass. The three and a half hours they had been feasting seemed to have gone in a flash. Justice and reward had been done to everybody. The sheikh had his beloved Jasmin returned to him; the Foreign Office, according to the newly promoted Basil, was over the moon. The Fenner girls had enjoyed yet another party during their short stay in Southampton and had also earned a sizeable wage packet each, by virtue of the success of the exhibition, in terms of their bonuses. Fenner was the happiest of all – he had won through with the success of Fenner Fashions International – he'd been welcomed back by Bootle's for next year's show. He also had been able to stand up as a man in face of his wife's and mother-in-law's antagonism, and he had secured a valuable sale from the sheikh's order. The sheikh and his party left amid cheers from the girls and best wishes to Jasmin, who had won her day. Fenner shook hands with the departing Basil, thanking him for what the Foreign Office had laid on that evening. Basil in turn thanked Fenner for his kindness in inviting everybody and told Fenner that if he was ever near the Foreign Office, to drop in and see him and with that, departed with a wave of his brolly. Mrs Fenner and her mother kissed Fenner on the cheeks in admiration of his efforts with their money and bade him a full and tipsy 'good-night' and supported each other as they always did and staggered to room 504. Tony and the girls made their noisy way down to the van for the ride back to the Lighthouse Hotel. As Fenner was about to leave, a waiter approached him with a silver tray, upon which was a folded sheet of paper.

'What's this?' asked Fenner jovially. 'A note from the management for all the trade I've brought them?'

'No, sir,' said the waiter politely. 'Just the bill for this evening.'

Fenner's body could not stand this last earthquake inside it. There was an explosion to equal three megaton bombs, as still clutching the foot long bill, he fainted like a stunned ox and fell full-length on to the sheep's carcass and lay amid the bones with his head nestled against the horns in the deep sleep of shock, looking like a mutton-covered Viking, who had been laid to rest on a bed of rice.

The whirl of the busy sewing machines in the factory caused Fenner to lift his head from his hands as he sat at his desk opposite Mr Thickitt. 'I can't believe it,' he said to Mr Thickitt who sat gazing into an open accounts book before him.

'Figure's don't lie,' assured the bank manager. 'It's all here and accounted for. I thought I'd come over myself because of the urgency.'

'But the exhibition was very successful – we took a lot of money. We've got the sheikh's order and that's worth quite a bit,' said Fenner on the verge of tears.

'Yes. That's income, but consider what you spent.'

'What I spent! I stayed in a tatty hotel and lived on soggy cornflakes and doubtful milk.'

'And yet the bill there was four hundred and ninety-three pounds, I have it here. Four nights for eight adults sharing, at four pounds per night per person – one hundred and twenty eight pounds, extras and room service and dog food – three hundred and sixty-five pounds, plus VAT and service charge.'

Fenner looked green as he shrieked, 'Those bloody girls were having things behind by back, they lived in luxury and I lived like a pauper . . . and I'm the boss.'

Thickitt looked doubtful, and read on. 'Hire of van and petrol and oil, one hundred and sixty-three pounds and seventeen pence.'

Fenner looked up. 'What was the seventeen pence for – the air in the tyres?'

Thickitt ignored him and read on, 'Wages, bonuses and extras, including overtime, modelling charges, food, tea and pennies for the toilets.'

Fenner held his ears and watched Thickitt's mouth move as he delivered the figures. 'I never thought girls could wee so much,' he said as Thickitt looked at him distastefully, then continued. 'Nightclub expenses, wife's and mother-in-law's accommodation and a 'Mutton Grab' supper at the Polygon Hotel – all total . . .'

Fenner held his ears again, and even closed his eyes this time.

'. . . pounds and ten pence.'

'The Foreign Office arranged that bloody Mutton Grab,' said Fenner, thinking he would drop in on Basil, driving a Centurion tank.

'They also arranged for you to get the bill,' said Thickitt coldly.

'I'll never vote again,' said Fenner looking a hundred and twenty years older. 'I've just paid off our National Debt. England would be down the drain if it hadn't been for me.'

'Didn't your girls have something to do with that?' said Thickitt, wanting to see fair play.

'They had everything to do with it, if it wasn't for them,' screamed Fenner, as his knuckles went white with strain, 'I'd have been a rich man, living like the Arab – what a great idea those blokes have with their women – it must be like that in heaven. They're all young and sexy – they stay in a special room, and they're not allowed to speak.' Fenner was shouting now as he ruffled the pages of Thickitt's accounts book.

'Yes,' said Thickitt, thinking, that would be a sort of heaven. 'Well Mr Fenner. I've been all over your whole expenditure for the exhibition and Fenner Fashions.' Fenner didn't feel like adding 'International' in case it cost him extra. 'And it appears that taking outgoings from income, you are one pound in credit, and so that I can close the books for this period, will you take this pound?' he finished as he offered Fenner the note. Fenner took the tattered pound note and sat in silence, looking at it forlornly. While he was sitting there in a daze, holding the pound note up before his eyes, Tony entered the office from the factory and, crossing to Fenner, began.

'Oh, Mr Fenner, can you ... oh, I'll take this for the office tea money,' and he whipped the pound note from Fenner's shaking hand. Fenner followed the journey of the pound note and then noticed Tony standing there. He didn't speak though his mouth seemed ready to; but that's how financial paralysis strikes. 'I fixed your wife and mother-in-law up in their office,' said Tony. 'Oh, and by the way, Paddy wants to see you about the rate of exchange in Arabia.'

Like a man possessed, Fenner leaped to his feet. Thickitt cowered back as Fenner sneered through his clenched fangs, 'Fix their rate! I'll fix their bloody heart rates.' And he stormed out of his office calling back to Thickitt, 'This is ... "The End" ' (he said cheaply).

HUMOUR

0352	Star	
300698	Woody Allen **GETTING EVEN**	50p*
398973	Alida Baxter **FLAT ON MY BACK**	50p
397187	**OUT ON MY EAR**	60p
397101	**UP TO MY NECK**	50p
397632	Les Dawson **THE SPY WHO CAME**	50p
397020	Alex Duncan **VETS IN THE BELFRY**	50p
398612	**IT'S A VET'S LIFE**	60p
398795	**THE VET HAS NINE LIVES**	50p
396245	David Dawson **VET IN DOWNLAND**	60p
397535	Stephen John **WHAT A WAY TO GO!** (see also Tandem General Fiction)	50p
397314	King Kong **MY SIDE**	60p
397780	Spike Milligan **THE GREAT McGONAGALL SCRAPBOOK**	75p
397527	Jack Millmay **REVELATIONS FROM THE RAG TRADE** (See also Tandem General Fiction)	50p
396237	Stanley Morgan **INSIDE ALBERT SHIFTY**	70p
398965	**RUSS TOBIN'S BEDSIDE GUIDE TO SMOOTHER SEDUCTION**	60p
397454	**SKY-JACKED**	60p
396954	Harry Secombe **GOON FOR LUNCH**	60p
396148	Keith Waterhouse **MONDAYS, THURSDAYS (NF)**	60p

0426	Tandem	
158350	Tony Blackburn **A LAUGH IN EVERY POCKET**	40p
136616	**DARLING – YOU ARE A DEVIL!**	50p*
157710	Spike Milligan **THE BEDSIDE MILLIGAN**	35p
157982	**A BOOK OF BITS OR A BIT OF A BOOK**	35p
15827X	**A DUSTBIN OF MILLIGAN**	35p
158199	**THE LITTLE POT BOILER**	35p
158008	Spike Milligan & John Antrobus **THE BED-SITTING ROOM**	35p

*Not for sale in Canada